Books by Thomas Walsh

NIGHTMARE IN MANHATTAN

THE NIGHT WATCH

THE NIGHT WATCH

THE
Night Watch

by

THOMAS WALSH

Little, Brown and Company • Boston

Published April 1952
Reprinted April 1952

*Published simultaneously
in Canada by McClelland and Stewart Limited*

PRINTED IN THE UNITED STATES OF AMERICA

THE NIGHT WATCH

PART ONE

THEY GATHERED ONE AFTERNOON about
four o'clock in the office of a detective lieutenant named
Frank Eckstrom. It was a conference that had been arranged several minutes earlier by Eckstrom himself, and
the three of them who had been summoned for it listened to what they were told in various and characteristic attitudes — McCallister restless and jittery as a kit-
ten on a clothesline, constantly shifting around, doing
something, keeping his hands occupied; big Paddy
Ahern stolid and doltish in expression, with his arms
folded and his legs braced apart; and Walter Sheridan,
blond hair shining under the ceiling light and Homburg
hat balanced carefully on his right knee, relaxed and
idle in the only chair in the room besides Eckstrom's.
From other offices around came a low hum of routine
department activity, long familiar to all of them; but in
their place it was Eckstrom who said what was said,
while leafing meanwhile through a voluminous folder
that had to do with another matter entirely.

Every so often an item in this folder would catch and

absorb him, and he would linger over it awhile, ruminating; but when this occurred he would be neither prompted nor interrupted by any of the other three, so that the initial details of this assignment were offered to them only in fits and starts, with long pauses between. They were given the name first, which was Harry Wheeler; the crime second, which concerned a bank robbery over in Brooklyn, with a guard shot down and forty thousand dollars in cash taken; and the complication third, but this again broken off by two incoming telephone calls and one long outgoing one. Then at last Eckstrom had finished with the other business, and displayed to each of them Wheeler's photograph. He leaned back in his chair, wheezing asthmatically, and looked over his glasses at each of them with an irascible and impatient expression, as if by now they should have understood all the details which in his own mind he had fully explained to them.

"Where was I?" he demanded, using a hoarse, tough voice — his ordinary conversational tone — that apparently had to rasp its way out of the barrel chest. "The wife, wasn't it? Well, she took an apartment a couple of days ago in that big new housing development near Riverdale. All right. We had the apartment wired this afternoon when she was out, and her phone tapped; and tonight I'm putting the lot of you in an empty flat up there on the same floor with her, but in another part of the building. You'll have the night shift on her, from seven to seven. And on days I'll have — "

There Sheridan uncrossed his legs, and with one palm rubbed his sleek looking blond hair irritably and resentfully.

"Twelve hours a night," Sheridan said. "And I guess every night in the week, hah? Swell. Thanks for thinking of me, Lieutenant. Thanks a lot."

Eckstrom, a bulky man with a big head square at the temples and bulging out dog fashion under the ears, regarded him with unwinking yellowish eyes.

"Two of you in the apartment," he said, going on with the instructions but watching Sheridan fixedly. "And one of you downstairs by the front door, in a car we're going to have parked out there. Now you can change off in it every so often, however you settle it. That's no matter. But when Harry Wheeler shows himself you're not to lay a finger on him unless you have to, because the only way we can get hold of the other one we're after, the fella who drove the getaway car, is through him. I hope that's understood by all of you. Is it? Or does Mr. Sheridan have something to say about that, too?"

Sheridan, recrossing his legs and resettling the Homburg on his other knee, commented there only with a thin, contemptuous smile.

"The complaint department," Eckstrom grunted at him. "Mr. Sheridan. I'll lie awake nights fretting about you. Now. Our man Wheeler is going to stay out of town for a couple of weeks, to see how the wind's blowing; but the minute he tries to get in touch with the wife I want him spotted outside the building, on his way in, so that one of you can ride up in the elevator with him. That's important. If you manage it — and if you don't I'll want to know why you didn't — the one downstairs will ring the street bell to warn the other two up in the apartment. And like that there'll be one of you behind him all the way in the elevator, and two more waiting upstairs for the door to open. Well?" He looked around again over the glasses. "Think about it a minute to see if you've got it straight — but only a minute. I haven't all afternoon to waste on you."

McCallister cracked his knuckles impatiently, nodded but said nothing; Paddy Ahern did his best to look knowing and wisely assured; Sheridan got up and fitted the Homburg to his head front and back at the same time, at a very precise angle.

"Then it's settled and understood," Eckstrom said. He took the folder. "And there's just one more thing. You won't forget the way I explained it, any of you; or you won't forget it with me the second time. I'll want you back in this office at six sharp, all of you — even Mr. Sheridan. And eat first. There'll be nothing for you uptown."

Then he went out, and Ahern stirred and spoke for the first time.

"Not too bad," he said. "I guess we've had worse details. Huh, Richie?"

"But maybe with better company," McCallister said, flicking Sheridan from the side with dark and scornful blue eyes. "Come on, Paddy. Let's get out of here."

6

Sheridan tightened the white scarf at his throat very carefully.

"That's it," he said. "That's getting the crack in. Good old Richie boy. A real prince."

"Ah, fellas, fellas — " Ahern said. He looked uncomfortable; he went out with McCallister feeling the same way; but still for that evening with Frank Eckstrom, and for several weeks after it by themselves, they had all to meet about six o'clock every night for the watch at 1775 Hawthorne Crescent.

Since it was Ahern's responsibility to drive the pickup car for the other two, he would be in the course of things sometimes a bit early with it, and sometimes late; but McCallister, the tensed up and overpunctual type, appeared invariably ten minutes before time on his Lexington Avenue street corner. He was a tall and thin young man with long arms and legs, a small head, high, restless shoulders and an olive complexion; and if he had to wait at all for Ahern, or for anyone else, his bodily movements and his quick and impatient side glances soon became nervous, high-strung and jerky. He had black hair, very dark blue eyes, a small, delicately cast nose and a narrow and pointed jaw; and due to the habitual uneasiness and intensity of his physical mannerisms he was known, by anyone with whom he had ever worked an assignment, quite simply and unmistakably as Itchy Richie.

If Ahern was more than a minute or two late on these occasions, McCallister would move around, mutter under his breath and light one cigarette after another.

7

Where was Paddy? he would ask himself. How was he behaving tonight? Had he stopped off in some ginmill to — No, he would insist. Not again. Hadn't he promised? But of course the idea would be present; and from then on, until at last Ahern swung into the curb for him, it would be edging and worrying at his thoughts. As soon as he had settled himself in the seat he would inspect Ahern openly, with particular attention to his eyes, and to whether or not he had a glistening flush high on his cheekbones. "What's the matter?" Ahern would say. "Nothing," McCallister would tell him, but perhaps after one or two grim nods. "Not tonight, anyway. Who said there was?"

They would drive a few blocks without any more conversation.

"Always at somebody," Ahern might say then, as if resentful about this. "Always worrying. And what for? I know Eckstrom hates booze as well as you do. And I promised you last time I — "

"So you promised," McCallister would agree ominously. "So okay. Then forget it, thickhead. But don't forget that I promised you something, too — I promised you next time I'd beat your brains out."

Ahern would mutter to himself, his dull little eyes furtive and rather shamefaced; and McCallister would settle back for the ride uptown, relieved for the moment. They had worked together then for some years, with McCallister's erratic moods of smash-ahead pugnacity nicely balanced by Ahern's more timid and cautious

8

temperament; and there had developed between them, sometimes with his usual petulant exasperation on McCallister's part, but always with a doglike and inarticulate gratitude on Ahern's, a deep bond of loyalty and affection. There was no sensible way for McCallister to explain this to himself — except that, intuitively, he received a good feeling about some people, no matter what their obvious faults were, and a bad feeling about others. Ahern, despite a clumsy body, a slow mind and a blotchy drinker's complexion, had always been one of the former, somehow; and it became no more than an unfortunate part of the job for McCallister, a detail to be endured night after night in 1775 Hawthorne Crescent with as much stoicism as possible, that Walter Sheridan was from the beginning, and without any question, one of the latter.

They were supposed to find Sheridan waiting for them outside his uptown apartment house at twenty minutes past six; but on most evenings he appeared only at his own leisure, moving in that graceful and erect way of his which would not have shamed a professional dancer, and always pausing in the vestibule to inspect his mailbox. He soon discovered that this habit of his irritated McCallister, who would immediately blast the horn for him; and so he did it each night, therefore, at greater and greater length. He had a wiry build, blond but somewhat bold good looks and a great deal of easy self-assurance; and he had been used several times by Frank Eckstrom to deal with women, and to gain their confidence. In these efforts he had been outstandingly successful. A quick, winning and playful smile, flanked by deep masculine dimples, lent him a persuasive charm of manner whenever he felt the need for it; and he used this charm often with McCallister because the instant and forthright reaction he got rather amused him. They knew from the start, of course, that they despised one another. McCallister betrayed this quite openly. Sheridan did not.

At a quarter of seven they would all get out of Ahern's car near the huge new apartment development of Parkway Heights in the upper Bronx. Their business from then on, or one extremely important part of it, was not to make themselves noticeable as a group to any tenant in or around Hawthorne Crescent; and so they would appear on that street only one at a time, and at the high point of the seven o'clock suppertime rush.

First Ahern would relieve the downstairs day man in the unmarked department car that was always in position on the left side of the street facing 1775; then McCallister would come briskly along and enter the building like any young husband on his way home from the office; and finally, a few minutes after this, Walter Sheridan would slip upstairs by way of the self-service elevator, and join McCallister in the dim living room at apartment 8E.

They found meager comfort in there for a twelve-hour nightly vigil — no lights permitted at any time, for any reason, and for furniture only a small wooden table, two

10

folding chairs and an army cot. In the entrance foyer there was an outside telephone, muffled, however, so that the ring was not audible nearby to any legitimate tenant, and in the kitchen and bathroom nothing more than the standard household fixtures. It was impossible, consequently, to pass the tedious hours from night to morning by reading newspapers and magazines, or by playing cards; and what the apartment had in itself to divert them was nothing more than the rich, shadowy gleam of newly finished parquet floors, the ghostly pale elegance of new and immaculate plaster walls.

McCallister, who seated himself as a rule by the big picture window in the living room, had a pair of binoculars with which to observe apartment 8B, the Wheeler apartment, on the other side of a narrow courtyard; and Sheridan, who took his place in back of the table, listened in on anything that transpired over there through a set of earphones. They were supposed never to make a sound when once on the premises, and to exercise great care when entering or leaving them; and so they would begin their watch noiselessly in the midst of all this newness and shininess that was illuminated, or rather partly revealed, by the courtyard dimness outside, slotting through at them in narrow colorless strips from the Venetian blind at the far end of the living room.

Now when McCallister had nothing of importance to watch through the binoculars, and when it was not yet time for him or Sheridan to relieve Ahern downstairs, he would soon begin to feel his effervescent abundance of

11

nervous physical energy fizzing up in him just as though a cap had been knocked from a bottle of soda water. He would prowl out to an attractive kitchen all porcelain and enamel, with blocked wallpaper and harmonizing linoleum, a brand-new white stove, a brand-new white refrigerator; after that, on the other side of the living room, into a short hallway with a bath and a linen closet opening from it; and finally, as the outermost boundary, into a bedroom with one window on the courtyard, and another, in front, overlooking the department car and the windswept December darkness just beneath him in Hawthorne Crescent.

It was possible to observe the central portion of the development from this window. Through newspaper and magazine stories, and before he had understood what Parkway Heights was like from personal experience, he had gathered that it was a new and only half finished tenant community financed by one of the biggest insurance companies in the country, and itself perhaps the largest and most advanced development of its kind anywhere in the world. The area occupied was at least half a mile square, with most of the streets curving down, eight stories below, into a landscaped section of ground known as Parkway Oval; and from the 8E bedroom he could examine many other buildings similar to 1775 in style and construction, all with oversized casement windows in the living rooms, and all either eight or ten stories high. The section adjacent to Parkway Oval, the only one to be completed and opened so far, seemed to be

12

almost fully occupied, because at suppertime the curbs below him would be lined by cars, jammed in down there with very little open space available anywhere. Lights shone then from innumerable apartments where housewives were preparing the meal, or serving it, or clearing off after it; and at the far end of the center, but angled sideway to him, he could even see a bit of the principal shopping area.

For a few hours after supper the oval was very busy — hordes of people on the move then, in and out, through the many apartment entrances visible to McCallister; traffic and activity everywhere, noise, commotion, something going on in all corners; and yet a short time afterward that early evening appearance of things would have altered radically, the store fronts he saw would be dark and deserted, the pavements empty and only the automobiles lined up bumper to bumper along the curbing.

They remained undisturbed there night after night, and all night. Free parking space within the development was one of the leasing inducements offered; but as yet, since the designated areas in back had not been hardened and leveled off, no attempt had been made to enforce the overnight parking ordinance. So at two in the morning, at four or at six, McCallister could look down on long lines of cars extending away from him towards the oval, with lamplight gleaming from roofs and fenders, from curved windshields and chromium radiator ornaments. The cars would be there, but no people — no people anywhere. After midnight he could

13

have counted without too much trouble the lighted rooms visible to him among thousands and thousands of neighboring windows; listen occasionally to a Van Cortlandt express grinding north or south on the Broadway extension, six blocks distant; and in all this abandoned night world of his catch only the echo of a step on the pavement at rare intervals, or the cough and rasp of a late car starting up back on one of the side streets. This period, when Parkway Heights lay safely abed, was always the hardest part of the night for McCallister. He would look down, muttering to himself and cracking his knuckles fretfully, at the deserted crescent and the oval beyond it marked by arcs of shrubbery every so often, and by the twin door lamps glimmering before each entrance; he would feel vaguely depressed, in the midst of all this suburban placidity, by the need for his own alert vigilance; and in the end he would have to return to the living room and Sheridan, although Sheridan was never the least company.

Earlier in the evening, when there were people still up in 1775, he would adjust his binoculars at the Venetian blind and fix his attention on apartment 8B — or else, and this with increasing frequency, on another living room that was set back to back against Mrs. Wheeler's across the courtyard. This room belonged to apartment 8A, which matched McCallister's on the other side of the building window for window towards Hawthorne Crescent; and it was occupied, as Frank Eckstrom had discovered in a quick preliminary checkover, by two

14

innocent bystanders — a couple of nurses from an uptown hospital who had moved in two days after the night watch on apartment 8B had been instituted. One of these girls, named Burnett, was tall, plump, talkative, excitable and altogether unimportant; and the other, a Miss Jane Stewart who for some reason impressed McCallister right from the beginning, small, dark, lively, competent and kind of fascinating.

The little one went to work every morning at seven, starting out then on her daily round when McCallister was preparing to finish his. She would dawdle out sleepily in pajamas at a quarter past six, and put on the coffee; look out into the courtyard to see what kind of a day was promised; busy herself in the bathroom for fifteen minutes; and at last appear again in a crisp white uniform, brisk and fresh, another person entirely, for her first cup of coffee and her first cigarette.

She had two gentlemen friends; or, at least, two male acquaintances who were permitted during the moving in process to hang up pictures, to lay rugs and to paint a couple of unfinished kitchen chairs. Each of them tried his best at various times to improve his status; but each of them, as McCallister found out in the only infallible way, by unsuspected and unhampered observation, never got so far as halfway to first base with her. She and her friend must have had it all planned. One of them never left the other alone in the living room with a persistent caller; and after the caller had left they seemed to be highly amused by him, giggling back and forth while

15

they attended to their fingernails for the next day, or ironed out a slip for themselves in the kitchen.

They were all right, McCallister decided presently, and rather puritanically — neat, pretty, intelligent, hard-working and straight as two pins. But of course he never expected to talk to them, even the small personality one, or to establish any sort of *verboten* contact during the job up here; and then a meeting came about between him and this Miss Stewart in such a way that even Frank Eckstrom could not have seen and avoided it.

It happened late Wednesday night, his third Wednesday in Hawthorne Crescent, when through his binoculars he was already beginning to feel deeply interested in her, and in her activities. He came in then from the street entrance after relieving Paddy Ahern in the car, and found the half pint and another gentleman friend — a new one — way over in one corner of the front vestibule, the darkest corner. It was a situation familiar enough to McCallister from his beat days, and nothing to interrupt so long as they were behaving themselves; but at once it developed that something must be a little out of the ordinary, because he was addressed anxiously by that girl: "Mister! Oh, mister!" just as the friend grabbed her by one wrist and whispered a few words at her in a threatening monotone.

A curious alteration came over McCallister's face; the small features drew in stolidly, as though tightening towards the mouth, and the dark blue eyes seemed to get harder, sharper and more distinct all the way around

16

each pupil. He went over there, lifting a forefinger at her in one of those authoritative, wait-just-a-minute gestures, and tapped her friend several times between the shoulder blades. "All right," he said. "Break it up now. Come on! I'm talking to you. What do you think you're trying around here, foolish?"

Because that was the one name McCallister considered appropriate, the friend being dressed in a long tan overcoat with padded shoulders, with a porkpie hat on his head and pinpointed yellow shoes on his feet. By this time, snarling back at McCallister, he had backed the little one around into a row of mailboxes. She looked badly frightened; but to McCallister, of course, it presented no particular difficulty — just a professional called upon to deal here in the quickest and most effective way with two amateurs.

"Make — him — let — me — go," she demanded breathlessly. "Please! He's hurting my arm. And he has no right — "

McCallister lifted another admonitory forefinger at her; then he took direct action by smacking the porkpie hat down and forward three times into the mailboxes.

"What's the matter?" he wanted to know after that, and reasonably enough as he saw it. "Didn't you hear me just tell you? Come on, come on. Out," he said, a little more ominous in tone now. "Out fast, foolish; and out this way."

There was a short struggle when the friend came around at him, swinging. But it did not develop into

17

anything very much; McCallister just caught the arm deftly the instant it started, swung it down and around and up back of the waist again, and in five or six steps ran the owner of it over to the street entrance. He had never done it better in practice. It looked like nothing.

"Now," he said, releasing his hold at the front door and speaking in a gentle and confidential manner, "I don't think I'd come back here and bother this girl any more. Do me that favor, huh? Just keep out of this neighborhood and save us all trouble. Because I can tell you something about yourself right now, foolish. You ain't liked."

"Pretty smart," the friend said. He rearranged a bow tie, his hands shaking. "You must think you can — "

"Look. Don't ask for anything." McCallister warned him, jaw muscles bunching up high there like small walnuts. "Just haul the ashes. Get out of here. Can't you understand what I'm telling you?"

"All I wanted — " the other said, backing off a step.

"All you wanted!" McCallister said, following after him. "Shut up! And I'm warning you now for the last time — get out of here before you find yourself spread all over the sidewalk. Go on!"

The porkpie hat bobbled away down the steps; McCallister dusted his hands together; and little Miss Stewart moved out from her place at the mailboxes to stare at him with enormous and still frightened brown eyes.

"I thought he was going to fight with you," she said faintly. "What did you tell him? How did you ever — "

18

But McCallister was greatly disappointed in her, and not at all averse to letting her know it.

"Wrestling in hallways," he said, looking her up and down with cutting appraisal. "That's good sense, all right. That's smart. What's wrong with you, anyway? You out of your head?"

"It's pretty hard to explain," she said, flushing a bit, and making some kind of small, miserable gesture with her right hand. "It was all kind of a joke, really. But — "

McCallister rang for the self-service elevator.

"Not my business," he said curtly.

"Well, it's mine," she said, flaring up at him then. "I only met him once on a blind date a couple of weeks ago. And then — "

The elevator came down. She flounced into it and pressed eight; McCallister, remembering Frank Eckstrom in time, followed her in and pressed ten.

"And then he wanted to come home with me," she said, the brown eyes snapping up at McCallister, way up, the head way back. "Because he knew all about nurses, the way he told it. That stupid, horrible — Well, I let him go out and buy sliced turkey and lobster salad and rye bread and I don't know what all; and after that I let him come home with me, or to the nurses' building in the hospital where I work, and not here. I went in first, if you want to know, because I said I had to watch for the night supervisor, and get her away somewhere; but then instead of signaling to him the way I promised to do, I just walked out of the back door and left him

19

waiting for me. That's the story. And what's so disgusting about it?"

From his bean-pole height McCallister considered her soberly and with more respect.

"You mean you got away with his food?"

She giggled behind one palm, eyeing McCallister rather flippantly meanwhile.

"The point of the whole thing," she declared triumphantly. "Don't you see? I ate his lobster salad and his sliced turkey for days and days; and every time I thought of him waiting outside at one in the morning for that signal of mine I got simply hysterical."

She giggled again, putting her head down like a ten-year-old.

"So he learned something about nurses," she informed McCallister. "Something he had to pay to find out, too. And it wasn't wrestling in hallways, either. I suppose he got my name and address from somebody at the hospital, because he was waiting in here for me tonight when I came home from the movies. Only if you imagine for one minute that I was afraid of him — "

The door slid open for eight. She shrugged calmly, and gave McCallister her hand in a very dignified way, very much the grand lady.

"But I appreciate what you did," she said, deepening the brown eyes until they were without question the softest and warmest and most expressive McCallister had ever seen. "Thank you again for it. Thank you very much."

20

She was still watching him with that admiring and tremulous brilliance when the door closed on her. How she achieved the effect McCallister did not comprehend; but there must have been something electric in it, since at once he felt a gentle and tingling warmth back of his ankle bones. She got to bed late that night in apartment 8A, first acting out her adventure excitedly for Miss Burnett; yet she was up again at her usual time in the morning, a quarter past six, when Sheridan was dozing on the cot behind McCallister, and when there was not another lighted window in the whole courtyard. No sound anywhere, either, he weary and dispirited after his long vigil, she yawning and rosy in a rough white bathrobe, and just nicely disheveled. It was at that moment when McCallister first got the idea that something extraordinary might be happening to him — something very extraordinary, as if he and this girl had somehow achieved a profound closeness and intimacy which set them apart from everyone else, waking and sleeping, in the whole world.

It was a good feeling to have; he wanted to retain it; and so he was still watching her through the glasses when Sheridan stretched and sat up on the cot behind him. He glanced at McCallister, looking over at the lighted window, grinned tightly and lit a cigarette for himself; then he lay down again, clasping his hands back of his head, and reflected on a matter that during these endless hours in apartment 8E had begun to occupy his thoughts more and more. Forty thousand dollars in cash,

Sheridan reminded himself, was what this fellow Harry Wheeler got away with; yet, at 1775 Hawthorne Crescent, there might be only he and McCallister and Ahern to take care of it when it came.

The gray eyes changed a little, watching the cigarette smoke idly — became absent-looking and yet intent on something. Not McCallister, he suspected; never McCallister. But Ahern . . . He smoked silently. He was still thinking about Ahern when the first day man reported for duty.

There was a phone call several nights later for Mrs. Wheeler just after McCallister and Sheridan had settled themselves. It sounded innocent enough, no more than a movie appointment downtown with a Dolly somebody; but of course there were certain precautions to be taken when anything like this came up. McCallister took them, exchanging a few words with Sheridan, and then going downstairs to tell Paddy Ahern about it. Presently Mrs. Wheeler appeared, walking off with that easy swagger of hers to the bus stop on Parkway Oval, and after that it was McCallister's responsibility to see where she went, and whom she met. So he left Ahern alone in the department car at twenty minutes past seven; and in this way the night watch at 1775 Hawthorne Crescent was cut off from any immediate contact one with another.

Ahern, of course, had now the cold, lonely and uncomfortable part of the whole job. He settled himself patiently for it, coat collar turned up, hands in pockets; and then towards nine o'clock a sudden December rain began to rebound from the hood of the car in hard drops, bright as quicksilver where light from the corner street lamp happened to catch them. The wind rose, whistling and blasting, and it got very cold in Ahern's place, with the ignition off and the car heater useless. One shot? Ahern thought. Just one? He shifted uneasily. He lit a cigarette and spat it out after half a minute; he stirred again; and then he told himself that nothing had happened around here for week after week, and that nothing would happen, surely, on the kind of night this was.

He decided on that one drink, using the arguments of a man who knew well what he intended to do, but wanted to justify it, anyway. How would Richie ever find out? And what difference would it ever make to anybody? But in the end, when he began to feel warm and comfortable in the Parkway Heights tavern, just around on the oval, it was more than the one drink; it usually was, once Ahern started. He studied his beefy red face in the mirror, observing with the usual toper's complacency his small dull eyes, his untidy long sideburns and his heavy mouth. Then he had a couple of more shots, since he'd had one, and noticed with a kind of foggy surprise how the neon lights in the window behind him deepened between each drink to richer and warmer yellow. It was ten when he got back to the car, chewing mints cunningly so that McCallister would not catch him out in what he had done. But it was not Mc-

Callister who was waiting for him then on the crescent. It was Sheridan.

"Where were you?" Sheridan demanded urgently, appearing at once from the apartment doorway just opposite 1775. "And what the hell were you doing?"

Ahern belched, covering it politely with his fingers.

"Took a break, that's all. You weren't worried about me, were you?"

"Not too much," Sheridan said, eyeing him sharply but covertly. "Only you better get some kind of a story in order, Paddy — because now you'll have to explain something to Frank Eckstrom. You know where Wheeler is right now? Up in the wife's apartment. I just saw him."

"Upstairs?" Ahern said. He turned towards 1775, almost comically bewildered. "But how could he? I wasn't gone more than — "

"How could he?" Sheridan said. He gave one or two quiet nods. "That's the thing, Paddy. That's what Eckstrom will want to know. I'll have to call him now; and I'll have to tell him how and why this all happened."

"No!" Ahern begged, the liquor warmth turning to something much different in him. "Give me a break, Walter. He'll want to know where I was. And he'll keep after me and after me until — "

He had become anxious and befuddled now, instantly; but he did not suspect that this was the precise reaction which Sheridan had wanted to induce in him.

"I don't know," Sheridan said, as if hesitating. "Who's

going to bust in at Wheeler up there and get the top of his head blown off? Are you — or me, either? No, Paddy — I got to call Eckstrom. But come back here a minute anyway. Let's watch that living room window and see what he does."

He drew Ahern back into the apartment vestibule. McCallister downtown, he remembered; only Ahern here to . . . His mind fingered hurriedly over that angle. Suppose he could handle Ahern? Suppose there was some way to . . . He glanced up at the windows in the Wheeler apartment, and his throat muscles tightened on him.

"He's turned the lights off!" he said. "He must be coming downstairs, Paddy. Duck back, will you? Let's see what he's up to."

"Then we get him leaving the place instead of going in," Ahern pressed eagerly. "We can handle him, Walter. The two of us can easy — "

Not yet they wouldn't, Sheridan thought, something savagely uncertain in him; not just yet. First they'd see. And then — A small figure wearing a gray hat and overcoat came out from 1775 and turned right from it, away from the oval, and back toward the next corner and the unfinished part of the development. A car in there, Sheridan decided at once, excitement blazing in him. And luggage, of course. And in that luggage . . . He dug painfully into Ahern's arm.

"All right," he said. "I never turned anybody over to Frank Eckstrom in my life, Paddy — and I don't want to start now. I'll take the chance with you. Listen! Get over on his side; keep behind him; but don't let him see you. I'll run up on this side and get him in front — and I'll go in at him first. Remember the way I'm telling it now. Stay back!"

He ran then, ducking low behind the cars parked all along Hawthorne Crescent. Rain lashed at him and at Harry Wheeler, who turned right again at the first intersection onto Narcissus Road. A car! Sheridan felt positive now. Why else would he be heading back here, and not out for a drink or maybe a cab on Parkway Oval? He raced on, still keeping on the far side of the street from Wheeler. All around them on this block buildings were still going up over a welter of contractors' rubble and a protective layer of wooden sidewalk roofs, so that he felt altogether concealed from the other man both by the darkness over him and the blasts of wind and rain spattering viciously across the road. He got past Wheeler at some point on Narcissus Road, crossed the next intersection before him and went on again when, in a splash of street light, he saw Wheeler still coming along with his head bent forward against the storm.

Where was the car? He determined, since Wheeler had arrived only a few minutes ago, that it must be parked at the end of all the others, the last one in from the crescent; and so he sprinted ahead until he saw a big dark-green convertible, spanking new, towards the end of the second block in from the crescent. He crossed to it, sheltering himself behind an oversized bulge of dirty canvas that protected something or other. He listened. Steps approached and then stopped; the inside door of the convertible swung open, flashing light over the walk. Crouched then, the big service revolver ready in his right hand, Sheridan edged around the canvas, placed Wheeler, and came up soundlessly in back of him. "Just like that!" he declared harshly, digging the revolver inches deep into Wheeler's overcoat. "Hold it! You ain't pulling anything here. There's two of us. Paddy!"

Ahern ran up, tense and agitated, but taking good care not to get in between them.

"Watch him!" Sheridan ordered, a little out of breath now, but steady as rock inside. "Watch his hands, Paddy. I'll see what he's got."

The first thing he looked for and found was the automatic in Wheeler's overcoat pocket; and with this, in a smashing forehand blow, he knocked Wheeler sprawling halfway into the convertible.

"See what he had?" He flashed the automatic towards Ahern, his gray eyes glittering and dangerous. "If we had any sense, we'd give it to him right now, Paddy; when they carry the gun we ought always to give it to them. The stinking, murdering — Turn around!" he said. "Up on your feet! What were you doing back here? And what have you got in that suitcase?"

Because that was the thing he had to find out first, the thing he must make no mistake about. The suitcase, a big one of new and expensive leather, was on the floor of the car, where Wheeler had dropped it a moment ago, and now Sheridan's eyes kept jumping across at it. "You know who we are!" he said. "So what the hell do you want? To see the badge?"

He hit Wheeler again, with his open hand this time.

"Or maybe we'll just take a look," he said, unable to contain himself any longer. "Where are your keys?" He snatched them from the convertible lock, fumbled through them and at last got the suitcase open. Quietly and in almost a detached way Harry Wheeler, a narrow-chested little man with a leathery complexion and perfectly opaque black eyes, called him the vilest of all unprintable names.

But Sheridan paid no attention to him now. First he reclosed the suitcase and glanced up and down Narcissus Road, while Ahern began to watch him uneasily, in quick side glances from Harry Wheeler.

"What's in it?" Ahern said. "What are you looking for, Walter?"

"Tell him!" Sheridan said. A nervous grin touched his lips as he slipped the police revolver back under his arm-pit and took Wheeler's automatic from the top of the suit-case. "Go on. Tell him!" His face shone either from sweat or rain. "Then I will," he said. "What's in it, Paddy? Nothing but his cut of the bank money. He was carrying it around with him just in case, you understand. Just in case!"

Ahern stirred, moistening his lips; Sheridan looked up at Wheeler; Wheeler looked down at Sheridan.

"A whole bagful of beautiful green gabardine," Sheri-

28

dan breathed, again betraying himself with that nervous grin. "And a guy that's in pretty much of a spot, Paddy, because he killed one of those bank guards over in Brooklyn. I'll tell you what he's thinking about right now — that maybe we'll take the money and let him drive away from here. Sure! That we'll talk it over and — "

"What?" Ahern said. He felt his heart begin to thump in him: "Cut it out, Walter! Stop it! I don't want you talking like that."

"Like what?" Sheridan said. He got up carelessly with the automatic, still grinning. "Don't get ideas, Paddy. I'm just telling you what he's got in his head. That's all."

"In *my* head!" Wheeler said. He spat between them. "Cops!" he said. " —— "

Ahern lunged at him, a sudden fury of rage exploding throughout his big, clumsy body, but whether at Wheeler's action, or the inescapable thought in his own mind, he was not sure. Sheridan caught him by one arm.

"Come over here," Sheridan said. They moved aside. "Listen to me," Sheridan whispered anxiously. "And forget him. Of course we'd be crazy to let him go, because a guy like this would only be waiting to squawk later. But I got his own gun right here, Paddy — his own gun. And nobody knows he came up here tonight — not even the wife, not even McCallister. See what it means that way? See how we got everything set up for us?"

He looked down at the gun quickly, and then in a sidewise, stealthy and significant way, without blinking, from the gun back to Ahern. Ahern stared at him. In one part of his mind he felt that he did not understand what Sheridan had just suggested, and in another that the meaning of it was crystal-clear, just held back from him for a moment or two. But if his mind remained curiously befuddled here, although he felt sober now, almost sick sober, his physical reaction was immediate and instinctive. He did just what Sheridan had done. He looked up and down Narcissus Road hastily, and saw shadows everywhere, the double line of cars parked back here for the night, the rain lashing away from them down the hill — no one at all out in this area and in this weather, and no tenanted apartment closer to them than Hawthorne Crescent, two blocks distant.

As he did this, Sheridan caught his expression and interpreted it correctly for what it meant — one instant, and perhaps only one instant, of wavering and temptation. But the muddy small eyes were beginning to show fright, Sheridan saw — unfocused a little, all jerky, under the thick brows.

"What are you talking about?" Ahern whispered. "You know —"

Everything came to a head in Sheridan. Get it done, he thought blindly; then handle him. He shoved Ahern to one side, knocking the awkward and ponderous body to its knees, so that both the arms had to push down and forward in order to support it. "Look out!" Sheridan said. "Paddy!"

There was one shot from the automatic; there was another shot as Wheeler started to say something, or breathlessly beg something; there were two more, poplike, muffled, as if the automatic had been placed against Wheeler; and then it became instantly and intensely quiet under that sidewalk roof on Narcissus Road. Ahern did not move his body at all — could not. What, what? he thought stupidly. Sheridan walked around in front of him.

"Get up," Sheridan said, glistening pale, but managing in this first moment a tone of quiet and composed authority. "What did you turn your back on him for? Were you crazy?"

Wheeler was now lying half inside the open door of the convertible, and half outside. His hat had rolled off under one of the front wheels. His right arm hung down slackly across the sand, with the palm curled back towards Sheridan and Ahern.

"Tried to jump you," Sheridan said. He made a vague, circular movement with the automatic; but in doing this he never removed the gray eyes from Ahern's face. "Tried to grab your own gun and give it to you. Well, what are you looking like that for? You saw how it happened, didn't you? You or him."

It was the one straw left for Ahern to grasp at.

"That's right," he said. He was still dazed. "I guess he come at me. But it all happened so fast, Walter — "

"Then get hold of yourself," Sheridan said. "Because you saw how it happened — just how it happened." Get

31

him busy, he thought; get him started. "We'd better lift him into the trunk and put a blanket over him," he said. "Come on now, Paddy. Take his legs."

Ahern bent; but then he shuddered and stepped back quickly, so that Sheridan had to manage it by himself. He did, afterward locking the trunk and walking around to Ahern. They stood together but silent; then Sheridan reached for the suitcase, and at the same moment Ahern flopped down quickly and placed both of his hands on top of it. They faced each other, Sheridan pale but quite self-controlled, Ahern moving the thick lips at him without saying anything intelligible or even audible.

"What are you doing?" Sheridan said.

"Leave it alone!" Ahern said, kneeling there with his overcoat open, his moonface dazed and bewildered-looking, and the rain beating in at him. "Don't touch it! You didn't do it for this, Walter? Tell me! You didn't, did you?"

"You saw it," Sheridan said, looking him straight in the eyes. "You were right here."

"Then why did you put him in the trunk?" Ahern whispered.

"Take it easy," Sheridan said quietly. "You're just a little excited, Paddy. Here. Let's get out of the rain. We're both drenched."

Careful now, he warned himself; step by step. He took Ahern's arm.

"You know why I did it," he said. "For you, Paddy. You mean more to me than a hundred of these guys, dead or alive. He'd have killed you without a thought; he tried to kill you. So all right. Why do the two of us have to get ourselves into bad trouble over it? Why do we have to take a chance on getting thrown out of the job?"

Ahern tried to concentrate, watching the trunk fearfully.

"You mean Eckstrom," he said.

"That's it," Sheridan said. "The big shot who never gave a break in his life to anybody under him — and never will. He wanted to talk to this guy, to get the name of the other one from him. You remember that, don't you? So he isn't going to like this, Paddy; he'll want to know why we had to get him around here, and kill him, stead of grabbing him in the elevator like it was planned. And he'll get the truth out of you; you know that because you've seen him do it. There's something else, too. He's already caught you drinking on the job once, hasn't he?"

Ahern nodded dumbly.

"Then you're all through," Sheridan said. He parted his hands in front of him, again watching Ahern covertly from his eye corners. "And me with you. He hates my guts, Paddy — always did; and this time he'll crucify me for not squealing on you, and for not calling him right away. That's what I mean. And that's if we're crazy enough to report it to him, Paddy. If!"

"But we have to!" Ahern said. He rubbed his mouth nervously. "What else can we do?"

"Use our heads," Sheridan said, at once quick, urgent

33

and persuasive. "That's all. We don't report it; we leave this car right where it is; and tomorrow one of us drives it downtown and parks it in a street somewhere. What difference does it make to anybody, only to us, if they figure he never came up here at all tonight? Think it out."

But Ahern was way past that point. His glance wandered a little, as if compelled, and fell at last on the suitcase. He shuddered.

"No!" he said. "You did it for that, Walter. That's why you shot him. And why you want to — "

"Are you crazy?" Sheridan gritted. "When I did it for you, Paddy — so help me. So help me! And now you're trying to make out — "

His tone was one of such passionate and excited earnestness that Ahern wavered a bit, and then tried to comfort and reassure him. They conversed in whispers, the rain slashing in at them, the wind whining overhead through a row of gaunt and uncompleted steel skeletons. Put the money with him, Sheridan suggested breathlessly; leave it right in the trunk with him, if that was the thing worrying Ahern. Because he hadn't done it for that — never! He had saved Ahern's life, and now he was treated as if —

"Then give me the car keys," Ahern croaked, wanting to believe this, wanting with all his heart to convince himself that it had happened in just this way. A great horror and a great darkness, not to be faced, was on the other side for him: that he had known what Sheridan meant about the automatic, and that he had consented to it by his own slowness and indecision, if only for half a second. "Just so long as neither of us touches that money, Walter. Will you swear to me?"

"Haven't I?" Sheridan said. "Haven't I told you and told you and told you — " He turned away, as if maddened beyond words; but the idea in his head was a much different one. How could Ahern possibly report this eight or ten hours after the event? There was no way for him to do that. So give him the keys now, or anything that would keep him quiet; and then put it straight up to him tomorrow morning, Sheridan decided savagely. Show him how easy it would be then to say that he was the one who had thought of everything; break him in two with it. He was unable to face Eckstrom now; then how could he stand up to him tomorrow, when through his silence about Wheeler he would have become as deeply involved in the whole thing as Sheridan himself?

"Okay, then. But I'll keep the apartment key," Sheridan told him rapidly. "I'll have to see if he left a note or anything for the wife up there. And look. You come back with me to the car now, like nothing happened, and wait there for McCallister. I'll attend to the rest of it."

They hurried down through the shadows to Hawthorne Crescent, and separated there outside 1775. The rain had stopped now; the sky had begun to clear; and unable to sit quietly and wait for McCallister, Paddy Ahern began to walk up and down on the pavement, feeling cold, empty and sick inside, and squeezing Wheeler's key ring in his overcoat pocket every few seconds. Had Sheridan deliberately used the automatic? And, if so, had there been time to stop him, had Paddy Ahern actually wanted to stop him? Ahern could not decide, and minutes went by while he tried to convince himself again that it was Harry Wheeler who had been responsible for everything, and not him. At eleven he came back to the car, stopped beside it and rubbed a sleeve over his forehead, taking it away wearily, and whispering some kind of petition in his head, just as an excited and white-faced Sheridan darted across to him from the street entrance at 1775.

What he said had something to do with that little nurse who lived next door to Mrs. Wheeler, the one McCallister was always watching. "She borrowed some ice cubes," Sheridan was whispering to him. "Some ice cubes! And she sees me upstairs just as I'm leaving the Wheeler apartment. I couldn't duck her, Paddy. I open the door and she's right out there waiting to — Can you see what that means? It's our necks! The whole thing has been blown to hell on us."

But this was another point the overwhelming significance of which Ahern could not grasp immediately.

"But she doesn't know you!" he said. His thick mouth twisted up clumsily. "How can she — "

Sheridan began to pound one of his fists against the side of the department car. He seemed in despair.

"Because who do you think Eckstrom is going to talk

36

to the minute he finds the convertible?" He glared wild-eyed at Ahern. "The wife! Can't you see it? And who do you think that kid up there is going to tell about Wheeler — because she must have got the cubes from him half an hour ago? 'Will you please thank Mr. Anderson?' she says. 'I'm bringing back the tray he — ' She'll see the wife sometime tomorrow, or the next day. And then she'll say about Wheeler, she's bound to after she hears he's been killed; and then Eckstrom's gonna get hold of it through the wife; and then he's back at us like a shot with it. Why didn't we see Wheeler upstairs like that kid did? Why didn't we grab him? And if we missed him for some reason, why in the hell didn't we call in on it?"

Ahern, understanding it now, felt thick nausea curl up and over inside of him.

"I knew it," he said, his voice faltering. "I knew something like this would — We got to report it right now, Walter. As if it just happened! Then — "

"Report what?" Sheridan spat frantically at him. His face had a white, blind look to it. "Don't you see it staring you in the eyes? Why did we have to shoot Wheeler four times with his own gun? Why did we shove him away in the convertible trunk and get blood all over it? What was I doing up in the apartment before Eckstrom got here, before we even called in on it? No! It's our necks, I tell you — unless one thing. Unless we take care of that nurse upstairs before the wife or Eckstrom gets hold of her."

37

"Take care of who?" Ahern whispered. "No, Walter! You must be — "

"Get her down here," Sheridan said, his face blazing up now only inches away from Ahern's. "Get her over on some street somewhere; and then make it look — Don't start telling me no, damn you! We're in this together, and I'll handle it if you won't. I'll get her out of that apartment tonight if I have to — "

"No!" Ahern said, backing a step off from him. "My God, Walter — "

"Shut up!" Sheridan whispered at him, his voice changing now, instantly, and his expression, and his eyes. "And get that look off your face. Watch yourself! Here comes McCallister."

PART TWO

Richie? AHERN THOUGHT. There was a cold flash through his mind, jagged as lightning; everything seemed to become frozen and still under it; then he turned his head and saw McCallister paying off a cab driver at the corner of Hawthorne Crescent and Parkway Oval. Sheridan, who had previously been facing the same way, adjusted the Homburg with both hands in a nervous mannerism that was the only one he ever permitted himself. "Stay where you are," Sheridan ordered quietly, "and keep your mouth shut. It's all right, Paddy. I can handle him."

He edged Ahern back towards the car. But in Ahern there was not Sheridan's iron boldness to face this out now against everyone; guilt, fear and shame gave him the panicky idea to avoid McCallister here, and at any cost.

"Let me pass," he said. He attempted a blind push around Sheridan. "I can't talk to him now, Walter; I'd only — "

"Yes, you can," Sheridan said tightly. "And you're going to. He's already seen us."

McCallister paused over there, his sharp blue eyes detecting them at once behind the department car. He decided immediately that a position as open and careless as theirs had no justification at all unless something important or decisive had occurred here during the past few hours; and so after glancing up at the windows in 1775 he loped across to them from the intersection in a great hurry.

"What's up?" he wanted to know, running his questions together, a habit with him, as soon as he was within speaking distance. "Why are the two of you standing around like this, Paddy? What are you doing?"

Ahern, groping at the first escape he could think of, dropped to one knee and kept his head bent as if fumbling over a loose shoelace. Sheridan faced him.

"I just thought he could use a break," Sheridan declared, looking McCallister up and down with cold insolence. "That's what. He's human, ain't he? And don't start barking at us the minute you're back on the job, McCallister. Nothing happened around here tonight. Nothing at all."

Ahern worked over the shoelace, his back presented to both of them; not a word out of him for McCallister, not a glance. That was the first extraordinary thing.

"Took a cab over from the subway," McCallister informed them, after a quick glance back across his shoulder at Parkway Oval. "I was afraid she might spot me if I came in again on the bus with her. Nothing happened downtown, either — but she's going to be along any minute. Back in the car, Paddy — come on! What are you doing with that shoelace, making it?"

Ahern said nothing. Sheridan pushed in between them.

"Sure. Snap right into it," Sheridan said, contemptuous and aggressive there. "Up on your toes, Paddy. What's wrong with you? Don't you hear Frank Eckstrom's right arm when he tells you to do something?"

Still refusing to turn, or to raise his head so that McCallister could see him, Paddy Ahern muttered unevenly:

"It's just his way, Walter. He doesn't mean anything. Leave him alone."

"Doesn't he?" Sheridan demanded. He continued to watch McCallister with contempt; but now, as before, he pretended to speak for Ahern's benefit. "Then he ought to get somebody to teach him how to behave. You should be with him in the apartment, Paddy. Up and down, up and down, up and down — that's the way he goes on all night. Enough to drive a guy nuts," Sheridan added then with heated passion. "And I'm getting fed up with it. You know what I'd like him to do right now? Get upstairs where he belongs, and take the McCallister jitters with him."

It was a deliberate outburst intended to fix McCal-

41

lister's attention on him instead of Ahern. It succeeded perfectly.

"What?" McCallister said. He was flustered for a few moments; then, being the kind of man that Sheridan had known he was, anger and indignation took over in him. He walked up to Sheridan, his features darkening. "Why, you dopey little jerk!" he said. "Don't start talking to me like that. Or I'll — "

"Or you'll what?" Sheridan said, without giving him so much as an inch. "Go ahead and tell me! Who do you think you are, anyway? And who do you think you're bossing around up here?"

"Stop it!" Ahern said, but in so breathless a tone that he conveyed to McCallister an almost intolerable emotion of strain and distress. "Stop it, the two of you. I can't stand the way you go on any more."

McCallister turned slowly to look at him.

"I'll tell you the kind he is," Sheridan interrupted again, his lips curling. "Always jumping on you, if you're once stupid enough to let him push you around; and then always keeping after you about something. What's the matter, Paddy?" He began to mimic McCallister scathingly. "Are you sick, Paddy? You act kind of funny, Paddy. What were you doing, Paddy? Did you — Why the hell don't you tell him you couldn't be sick — couldn't be! You didn't have his permission."

This time McCallister spun on him, altogether maddened.

"Are you going to stop it?" Ahern begged them. "Can't

42

you do that much for a guy, either of you? I got a headache that's like a knife in me; and yet you both act like
you're trying to — "

He got up and turned away from them, as if distracted;
and in McCallister an acquired professional caution, a
mental habit of concealing what he sensed or suspected,
or only half understood, dropped down over his first
reaction. Something wrong here, he began to feel; something badly wrong. He made an attempt to quiet himself; but the next moment, because Sheridan had already
forestalled him by that biting mimicry, he realized that
he could not ask Ahern the questions he wanted to ask
him.

"I didn't start this," he said; "and I didn't jump on
anybody. All I asked — "

But Sheridan had opened the car door with a graceful
flourish.

"You heard the right arm," Sheridan said. "Okay,
then; inside, Paddy. Double time."

"I'll see you," McCallister promised grimly. "And I'll
learn you some manners. You talk big around here, don't
you? Because you know — "

"Any time," Sheridan said, careless with that also.
"Any place. I'm usually around."

A bit flushed yet, and now ignoring Ahern, McCallister looked steadily at the other man about ten seconds
before starting across the road to 1775. "Richie!" Ahern
called then. He leaned forward, as if imploringly, across
the hood of the car, but there was an ugliness in McCal-

lister that Sheridan had succeeded in putting there. "Yeah?" he said. He was curt and uninviting about it. And again Sheridan got between them.

"Let him go!" Sheridan said, not as if he was advising Ahern, but ordering him, rather. "Why do you want to let yourself be all excited and upset like this by one of Frank Eckstrom's errand boys? Let him go!"

Ahern got into the car, slowly, without explaining himself or what he wanted; and after an almost incredulous moment McCallister tightened his lips and went away from there. Ahern watched him from the front seat. Like this with Richie, he thought painfully; and the thing only beginning! He put his head into his hands, not quite accepting it, while Sheridan moved up beside him at the car door.

"What do you think you were calling him back for?" Sheridan whispered, also looking after McCallister, but speaking in at Ahern softly over the top of the window. "Stay away from him! He knows you; and he can tell it on you the minute you don't act right. Why do you think I started that argument with him? To give you a chance to get hold of yourself. And even then you almost — " He gripped the window. "You'd better listen to sense," he said, putting his head in further towards Ahern. "I told you we have to settle about that girl right now. Because if we wait — "

Mrs. Wheeler appeared on the other side of the street, and from instinct Sheridan crouched low in back of the police sedan. Ahern kept his head in his hands, unaware

44

of her. He did not answer Sheridan. He did not want to hear what Sheridan had to say to him.

"I'm talking to you," Sheridan added tightly, the caution in his voice not quite canceling out another note of uneasy and driving urgency. "So don't sit there like a dummy on me! Wake up! That nurse had to see Wheeler upstairs tonight — and me, too. Why? Because I went and took all the chances on it, not you. All you did — "

"I never wanted it," Ahern whispered back from between his fingers. "I can swear that to God! You got me into the thing; and now you're trying — "

"I got you into it!" Sheridan said. "Sure! You never thought of the money, did you? You never had an idea that — "

Ahern shuddered again, violently.

"Just suppose we can shut her up," Sheridan said, quiet and grim now. "Just suppose. Then how is anybody going to find out that Wheeler was killed in this development? That he was here, even? Look. I'll manage about her myself, if I know you're ready to back me up on it. Are you?"

Ahern, moving his head from side to side as if in physical agony, showed him sick and terrified small eyes.

"No!"

"Then maybe you think you're out of it," Sheridan said, tightening his grip on the top of the window. "Because you didn't use the gun on him and I did. All right! But who stopped me? That's what Frank Eckstrom is going to ask you. And who tried to stop me? Did you?"

45

Those were the questions which had never left Ahern at ease for a moment since the thing happened. He groaned softly.

"That's it," Sheridan said, the gray eyes ugly and bright as steel. "Show your guts. You called McCallister back just now because you thought you could tell him the whole thing — your great friend McCallister! Well, why didn't you? Why didn't you kiss his feet and puke it all out at him?"

"Because I couldn't," Ahern said. He squeezed his hands together between his knees. "I wanted to — and I couldn't! And me and Richie were always as close — "

"And you're gonna be that way again," Sheridan insisted, shifting ground there as soon as he saw another approach to work on. "What happened tonight but an accident? Won't you ever see that? I'm tired telling you how it was — telling and telling you."

"An accident!" Ahern whispered brokenly. "An accident! Oh, my God!"

Stony-faced, and without the least flicker of emotion, Sheridan watched him from the car window.

"Okay. Talk to McCallister," he said; "and then see what happens. Damn you, anyway! I'll fix you for what you are. I'll swear to Eckstrom that you suggested the whole thing to me in the first place. And who'd know different? Go on and tell me! Who'd be able to prove different?"

"You couldn't," Ahern babbled. "No, Walter. You wouldn't try to — "

"Then don't fight me!" Sheridan said, clamping his jaws together. "Don't fight me! This isn't what we want any more; it's what we have to do to protect ourselves. You know that, and I ain't wasting any time arguing about it. Do you hear? I'm getting McCallister to back up some kind of a story for us without even knowing what he's doing. He's upstairs now, ain't he? All right. We'll have to use him some way. We'll have to think how — "

Ahern gave him a frightened, upward look.

"Use him in what?"

Sheridan hesitated. Then he brought out with a kind of strident harshness and finality: "In doing what we have to do. In getting rid of that girl. What else?"

"No!" Ahern whispered. His eyes darted around to both sides of the street. "You can't talk like that, Walter! Stop it! You can't even think like that!"

But then Sheridan was at him again — low, savage, compelling; and from upstairs, standing at his usual spot by the front window in apartment 8E, McCallister looked down on the police car, with Ahern concealed from him by the roof, and Sheridan no more than the back and shoulders of a neat blue overcoat. He watched Sheridan start away from the car, and Ahern get out quickly to stop him with an extended hand. They talked some more under the street lamp, Ahern obviously distraught, turning away from Sheridan, turning back, and then clutching his arm as if to beg something; then Sheridan looked up and McCallister drew back hurriedly

47

from the window. What was all this about? McCallister asked himself, now beginning to feel definitely uneasy. What were they talking over down there?

The discomfort became more obscure in him, and yet stronger also, precisely because there was no information at hand to suggest an answer to any of his questions. He went back to the living room considering them, and worrying about Paddy; then Sheridan came in, unlocking the hall door and closing it softly after him.

He did not say a word to McCallister; McCallister did not say a word to him. They had never liked each other; even during the longest hours of their watch in 8E they had found very little to say to each other; and yet tonight, with each of them studiously ignoring his companion in that silent and bare living room, it seemed to McCallister that a different and quite noticeable effect of tension was building itself up between them.

He was still unable, however, to put his finger on any reason for it. He settled himself at the picture window while Sheridan took his place in back of the table; a few minutes went by; and quite suddenly, with the instinctive tightening of the nerves that always comes with such knowledge, he felt Sheridan watching him from the other end of the living room. He turned; then, of course, Sheridan was not watching him at all, but blowing smoke rings in his usual indolent manner at one corner of the ceiling.

McCallister shifted his chair a bit, as if he was not paying any attention to Sheridan, either; but soon after he had turned around once more to the window he again felt the back of his neck crawling slowly and unpleasantly. At it again, he thought angrily. Watching me, trying to figure me out, maybe; how much I know, or how much I suspect. Why? What went on?

But there was no reason to point his thoughts in any one particular direction; impatient with them abruptly, and with himself for all this inward obscurity and uneasiness based only on what he considered a true instinct as to Paddy Ahern, he arranged one of the slats in his Venetian blind and inspected the courtyard outside through his binoculars. It had cleared off now almost entirely; scattered clouds and a milk-white December moon were visible to him far over the black and silver rooftop of 1775 Hawthorne Crescent. A light was on in the bathroom at 8B, where Rose Wheeler must have been preparing for bed; and next door, in the living room at 8A, Miss Stewart and her friend were throwing a party, perhaps a housewarming.

They were all girls over there, all young, all active, all talkative; and on the table, still partly gift wrapped, were two bed lamps and a set of red and white canisters for kitchen necessities. They were all urging the half-pint to do something, pointing at her, nodding, insisting; until at last, but with the prettiest air of deprecation and protest, she put down her coffee cup and began to act out for them some story or other.

She made odd gestures, talking away meanwhile from one side of her mouth. She pantomimed the shoulders of

49

the friend downstairs, the one McCallister had sent away so abruptly last night; she indicated the shape of the porkpie hat, and set them all screaming helplessly by walking off with two armloads of his food. That was really comical and well done, and McCallister enjoyed it. But then she added something, cautioning them that the story was not yet over. She went out to the foyer, and came in briskly, whistling to herself and snapping the fingers of both hands; and then she put a sober look on her face, and rolled her eyes way over and down in the right-hand corners, as if she was studying someone about half her size. Then, explaining again, she elevated her right hand as high as she could over her, and after that set her palms six inches apart and ran them up and up until she was on her toes. That did it, of course. He knew then whom she meant; the build, the height and the expression were all Richard Anthony McCallister to the life.

He flushed up, having always been on the defensive side about his toothpick physique; then he stirred and muttered, because everything that followed was either invented or exaggerated by that girl for the purposes of her story. She swaggered forward in a patent caricature of the way he had done it, pointed a calm forefinger at something, and with dead-pan ferocity banged the porkpie hat down and forward into the mailboxes. She yanked hard on the coat; she snarled toughly out of the side of her mouth, which McCallister was quite sure he never did under any circumstances; and at the end she

had the audacity to make that scene in the elevator ridic-
ulous, she on her toes with her hand way up in order to
shake hands with him, and he portrayed very soberly
once more with that down and sideways glance of the
eyes.

Everyone in her living room seemed to think that it
was an exceedingly humorous story also, but McCallister did not. He pushed back from the picture window,
mumbling; he got up; and then he discovered that without making a sound, or giving the least indication of his
approach, Sheridan had abandoned the earphones and
was standing directly in back of him. That was the last
straw for McCallister; never having been able to endure
people who moved too quietly, who were standing beside him, or more particularly in back of him, before he
was ready for them, he jumped away so quickly that he
knocked his chair over.

"What are you doing here?" he blurted out, the Mc-
Callister alarm bells recognizing Sheridan at once, and
yet, because of the unexpectedness of it all, shrilling and
jangling throughout his nervous system. "Who do you
think you're sneaking up on?"

Sheridan also appeared to be watching the living room
in 8A, and very intently, with his tongue pushing his
lower lip out over the upper, so that his good-looking
bold face had a strained and sulky expression. For that
instant he was as unprepared for McCallister as Mc-
Callister was for him. He concealed it better — and
much faster. "I told you," he said casually, "to watch

51

the jitters. Who did you think it was?" Sardonic dimples cut themselves into his flat cheeks. "Harry Wheeler?"

"That's all right," McCallister assured him, furiously aware that his heart was still bouncing upward and outward in erratic fashion. "I'll worry about the McCallister jitters. You worry about yours. Yours and Paddy's."

Sheridan had gone back to his table. In the dimness there the light of a cigarette went toward his mouth — and stopped motionless. "What are you trying to say?" he demanded. His voice had tightened up slightly. "Do you know yourself?"

"Beginning to guess, maybe," McCallister promised then, still all jangling inside, and because of that determined now to work on Sheridan instead of permitting Sheridan to work on him. "And I'll tell you what started me — when I came back here half an hour ago and got a lot of phony toughness thrown in my face. That was a brilliant idea of somebody's. Dandy. It must have taken a lot of figuring, huh?"

"Frank Eckstrom's right arm," Sheridan murmured. "The brain. I must have forgot for a minute."

"Like you forgot a couple of other things, too," McCallister said, putting his head down and forward between his high shoulders. "Never thought of them till I got back here again, did you?"

Pretending more than one knew was of course an old professional trick; and here, consequently, it was an indication of Sheridan's state of mind when he came out around the table at McCallister all tensed, white-faced and shaking.

"And then the big conference," McCallister added, working quite deliberately now. "You got rid of me fast — but you never thought I could watch the two of you from the window up here. That's another — "

"Then find out what it was!" Sheridan said, his voice rising passionately. "Find out!"

"As soon as I get Paddy alone," McCallister said, calming now to the exact proportion that Sheridan lost control of himself. "He's not going to hold out on me, whatever it is. He never could."

The simple truth of that statement stopped Sheridan dead short.

"All right," he said thickly. "Think what you want; and then go down and torment him again. You're good at that."

"Pretty good," McCallister said. "And you know why? Because Paddy knows I'd look out for him. Not for you, though. You don't mean a thing to me, Sheridan — not a thing. I'd as soon — "

Again Sheridan's control snapped; but it had been under very tight rein in him for some time.

"Then maybe you better ask yourself what Ahern means to you!" He leaned forward across the table at McCallister, resting both hands on it. "He was alone by the front door all night; I wasn't. So watch out what you're doing! You're not sucking anybody in here to cover him up. Sure, he's in trouble; I could see that as quick as you. But if you think you're pushing it off onto Walter Sheridan, either of you — "

He broke off there, panting after that recklessly insane spout of words, and from the pressure that had been building inside him for the last hour or so. And now it was McCallister who stopped short, thunderstruck for an instant because of the hating violence in this outburst. He still had no idea what the trouble could be; but he understood at once that if it had produced an effect like this on Walter Sheridan, it must be beyond question something of the utmost seriousness. But what had ever been serious up here for them except Harry Wheeler? Was it possible that — Then the whole thing came to him — complete, almost self-evident — and he moved like a cat, pinning Sheridan against the living-room wall before he knew what he intended to do with him.

"You caught Wheeler!" he said, nearly strangling Sheridan by the grip he had taken on his coat collar. "I'm beginning to see it. You took that bank money, and you let him go — and now like the cur you are you're trying to lay it all onto Paddy. You're lying to me! Tell me the truth about this, do you hear? Tell me the truth!"

Sheridan's gray eyes, the lips twisted and parted under them, glared at him. There were two knocks on the hall door, a pause, then two more. They both looked around at it. "Let me go," Sheridan whispered at him. "It's Eckstrom. Let me open the door!"

He straightened his tie and collar where McCallister

54

had taken hold of him; but McCallister stood rigid, his head turned a little toward the foyer entrance. It had always been his responsibility to look out for Ahern; that was the order of things as McCallister knew it; and there was no other idea in him at this moment but that he would have to look out for Ahern once again. Make sure about what it was, McCallister decided frantically; fix it up somehow; keep it from Eckstrom above everyone else; and then maybe — He moved back. Sheridan, edging around him, slicked his yellow hair down, settled his neck quickly inside the collar and opened the hall door, Walter Sheridan again after those hurried attentions. Eckstrom came in. Behind him, Paddy Ahern hesitated out in the corridor.

"I wanted to talk to you," Eckstrom grunted, just as rasping and tough as usual. "To all of you; and I got something to say. Come in here, Ahern. Close that door."

He moved forward into the room and peered across at the party in 8A, his big brown hat and his powerful torso, framed dimly against the yellow slats in the blind, floating erect out of lower shadow like half a body. He adjusted the blind so that more illumination came through at them. He turned. In this way, and quite naturally, he set his back against the courtyard window, and the three of them in front of it — the dim light is here now directed to their faces, and past his. As soon as that had been accomplished, he informed them with no preparation of any kind, and no emphasis: "The man's back. Our

55

man. I thought maybe you'd all like to know it. He was seen over in Leo Norton's place on Amsterdam Avenue at nine o'clock."

There was a short pause. Not even Sheridan broke it.

"And on the ride up I was hoping something," Eckstrom added stolidly, looking around at each of them. "I thought maybe you'd have him waiting for me."

There was another pause — McCallister to one side, Ahern over in the darkest part of the living room with his hands in his overcoat pockets and his shaggy head lowered silently, Sheridan perched on one corner of the table in a graceful and interested attitude.

"Back in town?" he said. "Swell! That what we've been waiting to hear, Lieutenant. He'll show sometime tonight — I feel it. Because Paddy and I couldn't have missed him earlier, if he'd been nosing around anywhere. We just couldn't have."

"My idea," Eckstrom said. He breathed against horn-rimmed glasses, and then began polishing them carefully. "Not the three of you — or was it the two of you? Ahern tells me that McCallister was downtown all evening after the wife."

"Just a movie," McCallister put in, husky about it. "We left here about — "

"I heard all that," Eckstrom said. "Mr. Ahern told me. You don't have to; just speak when you're spoken to. Sheridan. Where do you suppose our man took himself to?"

"I'm trying to figure," Sheridan said. He frowned earnestly. "Give me a second, Lieutenant. I know these guys; and I'm trying to think what — "

"But no immediate idea," Eckstrom said. "Like Ahern. Not a peep out of either of you. Not a hint. Well, maybe I've got one or two questions to ask now. First. Ahern tells me you never left this apartment tonight. Did you?"

McCallister wet his lips. It was beginning of course to take definite shape for him, with Wheeler back in town, and with Wheeler on his way up here from Amsterdam Avenue at nine o'clock; and the sickness and coldness in him, the way he avoided even looking at Ahern, were all growing more pronounced minute by minute.

"Never," Ahern said, his voice strained and heavy to McCallister — and of course to Eckstrom, too. "I already told you. He was up here all the time, Lieutenant. Just like I was watching downstairs by the front door."

Sheridan moved on his corner of the table.

"No," he said, as if happening to recall something. "That's not right. Not all the time, Paddy. I relieved you about eleven o'clock. Remember? The two of us were downstairs together when McCallister got back."

"So that's not right," Eckstrom said, achieving some sort of effect by repeating Sheridan's words immediately after him. "We've got that far. Good. Then who covered the front door? When you relieved Ahern?"

"Who?" Sheridan said. He sounded slightly surprised at that question. "Me, naturally. Who did you think? And nobody in the whole time — or out, either. It was raining."

57

"Raining," Eckstrom said. "At eleven." He had this trick of repeating tag ends of conversation when his mind was busy as to how they fitted together; and another habit of letting a pause go on and on when he wished to make some kind of a point without being the first one to mention it openly. He looked at Sheridan, whose throat seemed to go bone dry in one instant. Where had he slipped? How had he — "So I sat in the car," he said, giving Eckstrom a confident steady look as he groped desperately for the other thing. "And all the time Paddy was gone, five minutes say, I never so much as —"

"Raining," Eckstrom said, putting on the glasses but this time not looking at Sheridan with them. "Just before McCallister got back from downtown. Eleven sharp. That's funny. I had the idea it stopped earlier, Sheridan. I thought it stopped sometime about half past ten."

McCallister put a cigarette between his lips, which felt as stiff and awkward as if wads of cotton had been placed under them. "Got a match?" he asked Paddy Ahern. He went over to him and touched his hands for the matchbox. The hands were shaking. They slid away from McCallister's like wet ice. Stand up to him, McCallister thought blindly. Can't you hear what I'm telling you, Paddy? Stand up to him!

"Maybe coming down a little," Sheridan corrected himself, realizing at once that the rain had been a very serious mistake, since it placed him by the department car at a much earlier time than the one to which he ad-

58

mitted. "I guess it was like that all night, Lieutenant. Off and on."

"Off and on," Eckstrom said. He put his back to them; he looked across at the Wheeler apartment as if this was just something to talk about. Watch it, Sheridan thought coldly. Watch it now! "I thought he might have called her," Eckstrom said. He turned slowly. "He hadn't seen her in a couple of weeks; and I suppose he'd want to know whether or not she'd be waiting for him. That might be why he stopped off at some other place. Did her phone ring at all?"

Sheridan did not like that opening, because he knew Eckstrom; but he decided after a momentary hesitation that not even Eckstrom would ever be able to prove anything about that phone in apartment 8E.

"Twice," he said. "Once around half past eight; and once later. I think you got it, Lieutenant. When she didn't answer him —"

"I'll think," Eckstrom said, watching him openly and steadily now. "You'll listen. When was the last time he called?"

"Lemme see," Sheridan said. He lit a cigarette to give Eckstrom a good look at him, feeling careful in himself, and solid and sure as to what he could show or not show. "I guess sometime about ten," he said, seeking to cover the rain angle there by placing himself upstairs at that hour. "A little later, maybe. I remember now it was just getting ready to clear off. I was over there at the window when—"

59

"Half an hour late one time," Eckstrom said. "Then half an hour early. You can't seem to make up your mind about that rain, can you? Or can you?" He waited. Someone switched off a lamp on the other side of the courtyard, on an upper floor, and they all became shadows to one another in the living room at 8E. Ahern's breathing was just faintly audible. "I'm still waiting," Eckstrom said. "But take your time, Sheridan. We've got all night."

Sheridan allowed his mouth to compress in a surly fashion.

"I made reports," he said. "Plenty of them. And I told you somewhere about ten. That's it." His teeth came together. "That's the best I can do."

"When the rain stopped," Eckstrom said.

"Before it stopped," Sheridan said.

"But somewhere about then," Eckstrom said. "In that neighborhood."

Sheridan inhaled on his cigarette, and looked at it. He did not say anything. It had become obvious to him now that he was being pushed, and before he had any idea of what Eckstrom had in his head, into a minute by minute account of his whole evening. He did not like that. He did not like it at all.

"And Ahern didn't see him downstairs," Eckstrom said. "He didn't even see anybody who looked like him. What does he look like, Ahern? Can you tell me offhand?"

Ahern refused even to raise his head. Answer him,

McCallister thought desperately. Can't you see —

Sheridan took over.

"So okay," Sheridan said insolently. "So the guy stopped off somewhere after he left Norton's. You know that now — or you ought to. And what did you want Paddy and me to do about it? Run around blowing our whistles? You talk like — "

"Like what?" Eckstrom asked him, as if interested. There was another pause; nobody at all broke it this time. "Not a word out of the crowd of you," Eckstrom said. "Quiet as mice. Mr. Sheridan, though, knows he never left the apartment up here till eleven o'clock. Not until McCallister got back from downtown."

"Just before," Sheridan said tightly.

"Just before," Eckstrom repeated after him. "And that's the one thing you're positive of?"

"Ask Paddy," Sheridan said.

"I did downstairs," Eckstrom said. He looked out at the party in little Miss Stewart's, where coffee and cake were being set out now on the living-room table. "He could be still on his way," Eckstrom said; "or maybe scouting around downstairs to see if someone's waiting for him. I suppose we'd better make sure of that, anyhow. Take a look through the neighborhood, Sheridan; and let Ahern give you a hand on it."

Sheridan got up there briskly enough. But he suspected what this meant: that Eckstrom wanted to talk to McCallister alone because he was after something, or had already got hold of something. What? Sheridan

61

asked himself nervously. Where had he made the mistake? The rain? The phone calls? That business about not leaving the apartment? He showed nothing of this, however. "Come on," he said, opening the hall door. "You all set, Paddy? We been briefed."

They went out, Eckstrom looking after them in the light from the corridor. He had thick features, thatched blond brows, and a pair of protruding yellowish eyes under them that gave him an appearance of bad-tempered and stupid pugnacity. The temper and pugnacity were evident enough on occasion; but the stupidity, as McCallister knew, was another matter entirely. Now, as soon as they were left alone in the room, Eckstrom crossed to the cot and sat down on it, hands on knees and arms bent out a little at each elbow. He permitted another pause, watching McCallister meanwhile with those unwinking and froglike eyes.

"What's the matter with your friend Ahern?" he asked presently. "What's his trouble?"

But of course McCallister had braced himself by then for this interview, having deduced like Sheridan how and why Eckstrom had contrived it. "Paddy?" he said. He cleared his throat a couple of times. "I don't think I noticed anything much, Lieutenant. A headache, maybe. He gets them pretty bad sometimes."

"See if I'm able to guess when he got this one," Eckstrom grunted. "Not before you went downtown with the wife tonight. After you got back."

McCallister, sitting on top of a radiator with his legs

crossed and his arms folded, gave a slight shrug of the shoulders, and then whistled as if aimlessly through his front teeth.

"Don't know," Eckstrom said. "Can't say. Of course. Then forget it. But what do you suppose the two of them were lying to me for?"

The back of McCallister's neck got damp suddenly, and not from the radiator.

"What?" he said. "Lying to you?"

"At five minutes of ten," Eckstrom declared stolidly, nodding back of them at the outside telephone on the floor of the foyer, "I called up on that instrument to warn you all about Wheeler. I called on it five times in the next twenty-five minutes — and not once was there someone in here to talk to me. So Mr. Sheridan lied about not leaving this room till eleven o'clock — and the other fella's doing his thickheaded best to back him up on it. Why? Would you have any idea, Mc-Callister?"

"No idea," McCallister said. "None at all." But he lowered his head to avoid Eckstrom; and his dark blue eyes got small, bright and tormented-looking. They watched the floor from now on.

"At ten," Eckstrom said, "at ten after, and at twenty after, Mr. Sheridan wasn't in here to answer his phone; but he just claimed to me that he was in here to listen to Mrs. Wheeler's. You heard that, didn't you? Well, I threw it to him to see if he'd jump at it, and he did. It told me something. Something that's got a bad ring to it, Mc-

63

Callister." Quite suddenly his voice flattened out again. "Look at me when I'm talking to you," he said. "You're known as a close friend of Ahern's. Are you?"

But McCallister would not look at him, nor anywhere near him.

"I guess we get on," he said, putting his hands on his knees and rubbing them there carefully. "Always did, Lieutenant. I and Paddy — "

"Then he'd admit the truth to you," Eckstrom said. "He wouldn't to me. So I'd like you to talk to him."

McCallister spoke after a moment very slowly and precisely, as if picking his words. He had got all dark under the eyes, however.

"That's foolish," he said. "And you know it, Lieutenant. Didn't I just tell you that I and Paddy — "

Eckstrom shrugged.

"The more reason," he said. "You'd get it all out of him in no time. Where I'd — "

"No!" McCallister said. His voice rose. He stood up suddenly. "What do you think I am, anyway? Leave me out of this. I got nothing to do with it!"

"Maybe," Eckstrom said, very quiet and flat again, "I'd kind of like to leave myself out of it. As of now. Do you think I'm going to, McCallister? Do you think I can?"

"Then why do you ask me?" McCallister said, without very much breath in his lungs. "You got a hundred guys that could go down there and suck around Paddy, and make out like a friend of his. No, I tell you! What the hell do you think Richie McCallister is?"

64

"It's the job," Eckstrom said. "You know that. I never thought you'd have to make up your mind about it."

"So it's the job," McCallister said, just as quietly. "Okay. I walk out. Take the badge. Take it and — "

"It's going to be done," Eckstrom said, letting out a very deep breath, "because it's got to be done. You know that without my telling you. Now. I'm willing to let you do it the easy way — or I'll take him downtown myself and do it the hard way. Think about that for a minute. Then make up your mind."

Sweat beaded out around McCallister's mouth. It became skimpy and haggard-looking.

"Sheridan!" he said, pointing his right forefinger down rigidly at Frank Eckstrom. "There's the one. You know Paddy Ahern, Lieutenant; you know what kind he is. And it's Sheridan did all the lying to you; you said that yourself. There's somebody I'll talk to! I'll go down there right now and — "

"So you got the idea I got," Eckstrom said. "I thought so." He dropped his hands on his thighs, patted them, turned them over and looked at them. "Mr. Sheridan and that bank money. Of course. But I thought you'd have better sense, McCallister; I thought you'd see what we need before butting our heads into Mr. Sheridan's stone wall. He wouldn't tell us a word. But the other one — "

"Then will you give Paddy a break?" McCallister demanded huskily. "If I talk to him, Lieutenant. If there's some way I can — "

65

"Two of my men!" Eckstrom said, getting up then and buttoning his overcoat slowly. "Two of them." He went a couple of steps towards the hall door, and then paused. "Damn them," he said thickly. "And damn all the dirty money there is in the world. We're decent men in this job, McCallister, friends or no friends, or else we're worse than the kind we handle. And I'll give Ahern," he added, using now the deepest and toughest voice he had used all evening, "what he deserves out of this. What he's earned. You've got half an hour to talk to him. Get his story!"

He left, closing the door after him, while McCallister remained motionless by the picture window, his tight face rigidly pale and set against the courtyard illumination. Now the party over in Miss Stewart's had broken up; but now also, and for the first time in several weeks, McCallister had not so much as a stray thought for her. There was only one name in his head, repeated endlessly there, and without much sense — Paddy, Paddy, Paddy, Paddy! It shut out everything else for him. Nothing mattered at all beside it.

There was another apartment doorway on the opposite side of the street in the direction of Narcissus Road. Sheridan and Ahern had taken shelter in it. Sheridan, nearest the street, had edged out against the entry wall in order to observe 1775 Hawthorne Crescent without being seen from it; and Ahern stood off to the right with that heavy face of his lowered, and his muddy-looking

66

brown eyes roving around from point to point in a painful, miserable and furtive manner.

For the past hour or two he had felt nothing at all but a profound inward sense of darkness and confusion; and this because his one fine instant of decision on Narcissus Road, when at last he had understood what Sheridan meant to do with the automatic, refused persistently to place itself either before the shots or just after them. Even now he had no idea whether or not there had been time to stop Sheridan back there; or, and this was the important detail to him, whether he had really wanted to stop Sheridan. There were moments when it seemed to him that it could not possibly have happened, the nightmare quality of the thing making it incredible; and of course there were other moments when he felt distracted and overwhelmed by the conviction of a deep personal guilt. Now, in one of the bad moments, he stood behind Sheridan with his heavy features shaded under the hatbrim but deathly pale. They had not spoken to each other for quite a while; every so often, however, Sheridan would turn his head and study Ahern with sharp and calculating intentness.

At twenty minutes past twelve a man left 1775 and walked off towards Parkway Oval; shortly afterward a couple got out of a cab and passed in through the street entrance; and at twelve-thirty the party which Sheridan had watched earlier in 8A streamed out into the courtyard. They were all there — the guests, blond Miss Burnett and dark little Miss Stewart; and it became evident from their conversation that Miss Burnett was going off with two of the others for a country week end. There was much excitement at the last moment, their voices carrying in the after-midnight stillness around here; then Miss Stewart helped them with bags and packages, waved briskly and went back to 1775.

Sheridan watched her, the flesh wrinkling up around his eye corners in thin folds. He knew what the girl over there represented to him — and to Ahern also, if that mattered; but not yet had a definite course of action in regard to her presented itself, although the end was quite settled so far as Sheridan was concerned. The means, however? He was groping around that problem from angle after angle when Frank Eckstrom walked out of 1775, the square shoulders and the big hat inclined gnomishly ahead of the rest of him.

Sheridan drew back. "Here he comes," he muttered in Ahern's direction. "Gus Bruder just opened the door for him. Watch out, Paddy. They're headed this way."

For a few seconds the two of them froze in the hallway; then Sheridan peered out.

"All right," he said. He relaxed somewhat. "Okay, now. They're around the turn."

"I think he knows something," Ahern said, his small eyes jerking around and his right hand drawing his overcoat together with a fumbling gesture. "Or else he suspects something. I could tell the way he acted, Walter."

68

"That's because you have brains," Sheridan said, sudden and uncontrollable venom flashing in him. "He knows something! He suspects something! Well, let him suspect. How many times can you remember when you knew the guy who did a thing, and when you had to let him walk around laughing at you because you couldn't prove it on him?"

"He'll prove it," Ahern said, moving out to the sidewalk wearily. "I feel that, Walter — and I think I'd as soon end it now. It's in my head, I tell you — to go into one of the yards here and kneel down and put the gun in my mouth."

On the edge, Sheridan realized. Careful with him; very careful. He murmured to Ahern, most of his thoughts occupied with the other part of this business, that they were getting too jumpy and nervous; they were seeing danger all over where there were only shadows.

"Like that girl," he said, understanding here that it had been done the first time, with Harry Wheeler, simply because he had given Ahern no chance to protest it beforehand, and that it would have to be done now with Miss Stewart in the same way: "I don't think she'd ever know me again, Paddy; and I must have been crazy in the way I was arguing with you before. We're going to let her alone. We can still move the car tomorrow morning, and if we get that out of here I think there's a chance she'll never say anything to Mrs. Wheeler. You weren't worrying about her, were you?"

Ahern swallowed.

"Just the way you were talking about her," he said, speaking with much effort. "I was scared, Walter. It was like you meant — "

"I'm not crazy," Sheridan said, giving him a small, cold grin. "Not yet. Look. You get back in the car, and I'll go up and talk to McCallister. We'll work ourselves out of this thing yet, if we're just cagey enough to use our heads. Believe me, Paddy!"

Ahern nodded quickly, beginning at last to glimpse a faint hope; and Sheridan talked to him for a brief while, at last punching his forearm lightly for reassurance and trotting across to the vestibule at 1775. But he went down from there instead of up, groping his way across a cellar laundry room towards the back yard. All the buildings in this development were grouped around large areas which by spring would be finished playgrounds and parking lots, but were at present little more than sandy stretches of ground marked off here and there by piles of building equipment, or by red lanterns gleaming from open excavations and the sketchy whiteness of uncompleted driveways. He crossed one of these areas now, the one directly behind 1775 Hawthorne Crescent, keeping always to shadow, and on the next street cut back again toward Parkway Oval. He knew what he had to do now, because Eckstrom had trained him well in the use of quick and effective stratagems; and by the time he slipped quietly into a phone booth at the Parkway Heights tavern he had already decided upon a means of removing that girl, and Ahern with her.

70

It had become obvious to him during the past half hour that Ahern was in no condition to stand up under this very much longer. Then give him more, Sheridan reflected calmly; give him the girl. After that had been done he would have only one of two choices — break completely under it and put the gun in his mouth, as he had just threatened to do, or else deny everything no matter how long Eckstrom and McCallister kept after him. And if he killed himself?

Sheridan paused momentarily with his dime over the telephone slot. Wait a minute! he thought. Why hadn't he seen it before? The girl gone and Ahern gone; and the whole thing, once Ahern had used the gun on himself, waiting to be thrown over on him. It was Ahern who, presumably, had been alone all evening by the front door; why then couldn't it be made to appear that Ahern, and only Ahern, had caught Harry Wheeler by the street entrance, murdered him for the money and concealed the body — and all this without Walter Sheridan up in 8E having the least suspicion of what had happened?

It became instantly so vivid that he could picture himself facing Frank Eckstrom in an hour or two. "So we were standing by the car," he could say, very earnest of course, very upset about poor Paddy Ahern, "and that girl comes out and walks past us. Well, he gets all excited and funny-looking when she nods at him as if she knows him — but of course I never dreamt what he had in his head. I knew something was worrying him all night; I told McCallister up here, didn't I, Richie? But what it was — " Perhaps a pause there, a bewildered headshake. "So he says something to me about feeling all upset, and getting a drink around the corner; then he goes off after her, and that's all I know about it. Paddy Ahern! I still can't believe it, Lieutenant. What do you suppose happened to him? Was he nuts?"

Then even Eckstrom would have to explain it the way it fitted together, or seemed to. That Wheeler had been killed for the money; that little Miss Stewart must have had a glimpse of Ahern and Wheeler together, perhaps when she went next door for the ice cubes; and that in panic, when he realized the girl had remembered him, Ahern must have followed her and killed her, and then himself out of remorse and terror.

Perfect, Sheridan thought excitedly. He could claim that he had left 8E for a cup of coffee about ten o'clock, and that Ahern had been on watch there at that time; and so, as Eckstrom reconstructed it, it would have to be Ahern who had seen Wheeler in the wife's place. So Ahern had gone around there, and taken him out, and the girl had seen them, and all her friends at that party would have to corroborate that she had gone next door at one time, without of course knowing anything about the people she had seen there. So let him use the gun on himself, Sheridan decided now; or, if it came to that, let him be given a little bit of help on it. Get the car keys from him first, of course; hide the money somewhere; and then who could say that Wheeler had been carrying the money with him, who could ever find out what had happened to it?

He took a deep breath, closed his eyes for a moment, thought about it some more, and then dialed Information. At ten minutes of one, through her, he had little Miss Stewart on the other end of the line. His story was all prepared for her also. An accident, Sheridan told her, making his voice properly impressive and official; a very bad accident over on Broadway. Three girls riding together in a private car had been hurt, and one of them had given the police this number to call before she lost consciousness. A Miss Burnett. Was it —

"Molly?" Miss Stewart said, staring wide-eyed now at the foyer wall up in apartment 8A. "Oh, no! They just left here a couple of minutes ago. They couldn't have — "

"I'm afraid this just happened," Sheridan put in stolidly. He gave the name of the hospital; he said that he was a Sergeant Murphy, and that he'd be waiting for her in the emergency ward if she came over as quickly as she could.

"Of course," little Miss Stewart whispered breathlessly. "Yes. I'll be there right away. Thank you."

So it was all managed that simply. At twelve-thirty, Sheridan knew, the last development bus left Parkway Heights for the subway station six blocks distant; and on the oval at this time of night there would be almost no chance of coming across a stray taxicab. Parkway Heights got up early, and went to bed early, so that it was not any kind of a prospect for nighthawk cabbies.

73

How would that girl get to the hospital, then? On foot, Sheridan had decided, over to the subway station; no other transportation available to her if things went as they should. He was aware, furthermore, that only one street ran east from the development over to Broadway, and now he headed for it.

The name was Eckington Street, and the thoroughfare itself was straight, wide and deserted at this hour. He reached it at a few minutes to one, long before Miss Stewart, and moved cautiously ahead past advertising billboards, and empty fields that were littered everywhere by weeds and rubbish. As soon as the development had dropped behind him, the region became one of almost indescribable suburban ugliness — but of course suited in what it was, and suited admirably, for Sheridan's purpose. Civic pride had constructed Eckington Street in an optimistic year; progress, for some mysterious reason, had bypassed and ignored it; and now over the roadway, and the desolate fields flanking it, there was always a burnt rubbery smell, a haze by day, and a dank and low-lying mist by night. On empty lots cars had been abandoned to time and weather, with most of the fenders missing, and worn upholstery coiling out from doors that hung jaggedly alop by one hinge. Tires had been heaped up, and scrap metal and refuse dumped and forgotten, behind the billboards; and only an occasional one-family house, squatting apart as if sullenly isolated from its few neighbors, had been erected on this patch of damp rot set down for block after block

74

outside the sparkling and lofty magnificence of Parkway Heights.

Sheridan ran on under a railroad trestle. Would she be able to find a taxi back there? Or would she know someone in the house who might be persuaded to give her a lift? Those possibilities nagged at him; but then he felt that after all his timing and thinking matters would not be permitted to work out for him in such a cruelly unfair way. Three blocks in, when he was halfway along Eckington Street, and on the darkest and most isolated part of it, he paused under one of the billboards. The one light shining over him at the far corner swung fit-fully against the night wind; and somewhere across the fields a tiny and mysterious fire could be glimpsed flam-ing in the heart of all this desolation. Here, Sheridan told himself. Right here. He ducked quickly back under the billboard, back into weeds and heavy shadow; and after that there was nothing alive, or at any rate nothing moving and visible, all the way from one end of Ecking-ton Street to the other.

PART THREE

RICHIE MCCALLISTER had come down-
stairs in the self-service elevator at twenty of one. He
consequently missed Sheridan in the front hall at 1775
by about two minutes or so, but without suspecting it;
all he sensed, in glancing around the green and gold
entrance lobby, was a late-at-night feeling of stillness
and isolation, as if no one had passed this way for some
time. He want ahead to the glass and ironwork front
door, peered out through it and saw Paddy Ahern sitting across from him in the department car. He worked
his lips slightly, watching Ahern; and after this he put
his hand on the doorknob, started to turn it, hesitated —
and hesitated again.

He did this for the reason that always before it had
been his part to protect Ahern, to bully and berate him
occasionally in private, and for the good of his soul; but
also, and whenever anyone else was concerned, to take
up for him in the forthright and belligerent McCallister
way even with Frank Eckstrom himself. No one, so long
as McCallister was within hearing, had been able to

express amused superiority at Ahern's slowness of thought, or of his uneasy caution in moments of physical crisis; and yet tonight it seemed plain that little could be done for him, even by McCallister, until the truth was admitted — and perhaps not then. That was the hard point to grasp here: his own helplessness if Ahern had actually become involved in anything serious. It was why he paused again on the front steps, feeling a personal shame at what Eckstrom had asked him to do, and bothered by a persistent conviction that if he could not help Ahern in this matter he should at least refuse to betray him. He fought that out with himself, his expression as set and rigid as it had been with Eckstrom in the living room at 8E; and after he had approached the department car his nervous physical mannerisms became much more emphasized, and jerkier than ever.

Ahern had not yet seen him. He stopped, twisting his small head from one side to the other, looking around for Sheridan, and punching his fists up and forward in his overcoat pockets; but he did not say anything to announce his presence until Ahern, spotting him at last behind the department car, stared back at him and then got out hurriedly.

He looked very bad, McCallister saw — his mouth jumpy on him, his eyes bloodshot, his expression hunted and uneasy under the street lamp. "I been hoping you'd come down," he said, advancing in a humble and timid fashion, and searching McCallister's face anxiously, going over and over it. "I thought maybe you were sore

77

at me. Were you?" His voice pleaded with McCallister. "Were you, Richie?"

There was an effect of contraction and dry heat behind McCallister's palate somewhere.

"No," he said. He found himself speaking with some effort. "What for?"

"The way we were talking to you," Ahern said. "Me and Sheridan."

"That's all right," McCallister said.

"But I felt kind of bad about it," Ahern confessed — low, unsteadily. "You know what I think of you, Richie; you're like my own brother. That's why I — "

Stop it, McCallister thought. Stop it! He walked three or four steps away.

"What's the matter?" Ahern said, overanxious at once then. "Richie!"

He came up to McCallister and took his arm; and after that there was no impersonal and painless way for McCallister to do it. "Keep your hands off me!" he ordered breathlessly. He knocked them off. "That's the matter. Don't touch me!"

"Oh!" Ahern said. A sallow crease folded in at each side of his mouth; but never had he defended himself against McCallister — never argued anything, never questioned. "Sure," he said quietly. "Okay, Richie. I only wanted to — "

"Richie!" McCallister said, the thing started now, and no other idea in him but to finish it as quickly as possible. "Richie! What do you suppose that means any more?

What do you think it's going to get you?" His tone became passionate; his dark blue eyes glittered. "Nothing!" he said, putting his face close to Ahern. "Are you stupid enough to think that you're fooling anybody about this, you and Sheridan? Are you?"

"About this?" Ahern babbled. "About what?" His heavy lips quivered. "What do you mean? What are you saying, Richie?"

"Go on!" McCallister grated at him, and in the most direct, brutal and contemptuous manner. "Start lying to me. Swear yourself away again like you just did upstairs with Frank Eckstrom. Tell me what you were doing around here, and what Sheridan was doing — and lie, lie, lie! Go ahead. I'm waiting for it. I came down here expecting it."

It was the next move in the process he had decided upon; he had never suspected that it would be also the last. Ahern stared at him; then, quite suddenly, Ahern clasped his hands in an agonized but oddly devout gesture, swung away from him, and swung back.

"You never left the car," McCallister said thickly, "and that dirty bastard Sheridan never left the apartment. You never saw Wheeler, either of you. And you never made a deal with him for the bank money, so that — "

"Don't say it!" Ahern whispered at him. "Don't, Richie!"

"Then admit it," McCallister almost shouted, the thing nearly done now, and no more pity in him for

79

Ahern than for himself. "Admit it to me! You took his dirty blood money and let him walk out of here because you thought no one was going to find out about it. Answer me! Isn't that what you did? Isn't it?"

"I can't," Ahern said, distracted now, and making an inarticulate outward motion of both hands at McCallister. "I can't tell you, Richie! I tried before, when you were down here. And I — "

"Don't touch me," McCallister warned him. "You let him go, didn't you? You and Sheridan got him while I was gone. Answer me!" He took Ahern by both coat lapels. He shook him.

"Let him go!" Ahern whispered. He smiled horribly. "No, Richie. That wasn't it. That wasn't the smart way. So what we did — "

He tore away from McCallister, putting his hands up suddenly over his face, over his eyes. But it did not have to be finished in words then for McCallister; what they had done to Harry Wheeler became plain and unmistakable in the tremendous overhang of that last sentence.

"What?" McCallister whispered at him. "Paddy!" He turned chalk-white; he made a convulsive movement of the head, his eyes fixed on Ahern, and stepped back from him just as Ahern, a couple of hours ago, had stepped back from Walter Sheridan.

"Now you know it," Ahern said. He began to breathe heavily; a violent shudder went through him. "Walter saw him upstairs," he added, with a groping gesture

80

back towards 1775. "Then he comes down and we get him around by his car on Narcissus Road, a couple of blocks in, and he tries to grab my own gun and use it on me. And Walter shot him. He had to. That was how it was, Richie! Everything!"

"Are you trying to say that you only protected your-selves?" McCallister breathed after a paralyzed second or two. "No! That can't be the truth, Paddy. You knew you had to report something like this. You knew it!"

But there again was the treacherous ground for Ahern — the instant of temptation, and all the subsequent darkness, confusion and mental anguish. He beat the air with his right fist, trying to convince himself as well as McCallister.

"I'm telling you it was Wheeler or me, Richie — Wheeler or me!"

"And I believe you," McCallister said, giving him one or two incredulous nods. "If you say so, Paddy, I'm ready to — But the money! What about that? That's what Eckstrom will ask you. Was it in the car with him? Did you see it?"

"In the trunk," Ahern croaked. "We never touched it, Richie. We left it with him."

"But you knew where it was," McCallister said, a great stiffness and deadness beginning to spread through him. "And you left it in the one place where it would be safe for the two of you until you could go back and get it tomorrow morning. That's what it was. That's why you — "

81

"No!" Ahern said, wringing his hands again. "Don't put it together that way, Richie! Please!"

"What way?" McCallister demanded huskily. "The way Eckstrom's going to see it — the only way he can see it? Holy God, Paddy! Don't you understand what this is yet — what it means? Who wanted to leave that money in the car with him, you or Sheridan? Who thought it up and suggested it?"

Ahern, shaking his head dumbly, passed both hands upward over his face that was now dazzled and glassy-looking, as if he could not understand how or why the truth had come out of him.

"I don't know. I can't remember any more. Walter, maybe." He attempted a more coherent explanation. "He said Eckstrom would break the two of us for the way we'd handled it. I'd been drinking, Richie. And Sheridan thought — "

"How did it start?" McCallister interrupted him. "You've got to tell me, Paddy! How did it happen?"

"He'd been talking funny," Ahern whispered. "How no one knew Wheeler came up here. How we could easy — " He gave another uncontrollable shiver. "But it was like I couldn't understand what he meant, Richie — not all at once. Then he knocks me down into the sand. 'Watch out,' he hollers. And it's all over! And he says didn't I see it — how Wheeler tried to come at me, how it happened. And I says sure, I did. Because I was afraid of him then, Richie. He's staring at me like he hates me. 'Yes,' I says, 'I saw him.' I — "

McCallister's arms had become rigid, holding Ahern away from him.

"You mean he wanted to do it? He set it up deliberately?"

"I don't know," Ahern whispered brokenly. "God help me, Richie. I couldn't tell you."

"Did he use a gun?" McCallister demanded, his mind racing to apportion the blame here as Frank Eckstrom would understand it. "His own gun?"

Again Ahern had to concentrate.

"No. The automatic he had — Wheeler's automatic. And now I keep thinking that it was my fault, maybe, that I could have stopped him. I wish I was dead," he whispered, squeezing his eyes shut. "I wish I'd taken my gun when I wanted to, and — "

"Paddy, Paddy!" McCallister said. He put an arm around Ahern's shoulders, his throat almost closing up on him. "You can't even think of that! We'll tell Eckstrom — that's the first thing. Because he knows you and he knows Sheridan; and he'll see this the way I see it, or I'll make him."

"If you'll stay with me," Ahern whispered, his face glistening. "Will you, Richie? I'm going to need you. I'm all — "

"Did I ever go back on you?" McCallister asked unsteadily. "Did I? You know better, Paddy."

Ahern made some attempt to compose himself then, and on the other side of the street Miss Stewart appeared from 1775, running out from the courtyard and glancing

83

right and left of her as if for a taxicab. McCallister saw
and recognized her because he happened to be facing
that way. Ahern did not.

"I'll be all right then," Ahern said, the long sideburns
looking very dark and shaggy against his cheeks. "If
you're here. I'm even glad now it's over with — out of
me."

Over with! McCallister thought. He forgot little Miss
Stewart.

"Tell your story," he said. "That's all, Paddy." Again
his throat dried up on him; he had to clear it. "Eckstrom
will be able to see how Sheridan talked you into this.
How he figured out everything right from the beginning."

"Many a night," Ahern said dully, "you and I waited
like this for Frank Eckstrom. Hah, Richie? Never no
more, though. And you don't have to make out about it,
because I know." He looked up at McCallister now, with
those ugly features of his, never made for such things,
almost tranquil from an expression of the utmost gentle-
ness and affection; then he glanced down the quiet half
circle of Hawthorne Crescent, and just missed little Miss
Stewart as she rounded the corner there and hurried on
into the oval.

"I'm through, Richie," he added quietly, as if he had
found somewhere that final resource of personal dignity
that comes often to a man when he understands at last
that there is nothing to be done for him. "You know it,
but you won't say it — because you always had some-

84

thing fine and decent in you — and you always will, too. I'm not gonna forget that, whatever happens to me. I'm gonna think of the times when we used to —"

McCallister walked several paces away from him, keeping his back turned. "Will you stop?" he said then. "Will you shut up for a minute, Paddy?"

"All right," Ahern said, his voice under much better control now than McCallister's. "But there's one thing I'd like you to know. I wouldn't let him touch that money, Richie. Or that girl, either, when he started talking about her. Because —"

Then he caught himself. Bad enough now, he thought heavily; why bring the girl in, and make it worse?

McCallister kept his eyes fixed on the corner of Narcissus Road. A girl? he asked himself. What girl? It did not seem very important for a moment; but then a bothersome and unpleasant recollection was thrown into sharp focus for him — he at the picture window in 8E, watching through the binoculars, Sheridan coming up soundlessly behind him and watching also, the gray eyes not boyish at all then on Miss Stewart, the mouth with that strained and sulky expression on it. He turned back to Ahern.

"What girl are you talking about?" he demanded.

"Let it go," Ahern said. "Please, Richie. Just forget it."

But for some reason McCallister glanced down towards the oval. He did not see Miss Stewart down there — or Sheridan, either.

85

"Then where is he?" he said. "What's he doing, Paddy?"

Ahern took off his hat and rubbed his forehead wearily.

"He's upstairs," he said. "Didn't you see him? Didn't you talk to him?"

"Upstairs where?" McCallister said, the thing indicated for him now, but without any detailed coherence. "I tell you he isn't — and I know. I just come down. And there's one thing I noticed about him: just a couple of hours ago I caught him staring over at that little nurse in 8A with a kind of funny look on his face. That's why I — "

Ahern hesitated, looking at him.

"Leave it alone," he said then. "Will you please, Richie?"

"But I want to know!" McCallister repeated doggedly. "Did she have anything to do with him, Paddy — with this whole thing? Because she just ran out of the house here. I thought you saw her."

Ahern moistened his lips; then he moved a couple of steps into the road, facing Parkway Oval. Ran out of the house? he thought. Why? And where was Sheridan?

"I think she saw him in the Wheeler apartment," he said, looking around at McCallister after a moment with a distressed narrowing of the eyes. "That's what he told me, anyway. And at first he was talking about how we should — "

Again he caught himself.

"Are you trying to say that he was afraid of her?" Mc-

Callister asked incredulously, the symbols of motive and countermotive no more than shorthand as yet, but his knowledge of Walter Sheridan bringing them almost at once into some kind of workable equation. "That he thought she might tell Eckstrom or somebody where she saw him?"

"But he wouldn't try anything," Ahern said. He was sweating. "We talked it over, Richie. And I made him —"

"Then where is he?" McCallister said. "Why did he lie to you about going upstairs?"

Ahern ran out into the road. McCallister, tearing himself free from a momentary paralysis, sprinted past him to the corner of Parkway Oval. What he saw from there were just the street lights curving out and then in around the murmurous darkness of the central green; an apartment window high up here and there, shining like muzzy gold against the transparent blackness of the night air; and the twin door lamps that gleamed away from him at entry after entry, each vestibule with its two steps up, its chaste colonial handrail and its softly illuminated house number. No Miss Stewart anywhere. No Sheridan. The bus stop across from him, marked off by a section of curb set between upright metal stanchions, lay deserted; but on the same corner a man with two piles of morning tabloids arranged on top of a wooden box blew on his hands and stamped his feet on the pavement in order to warm them. Then Ahern, using his head here where McCallister had not, got the department car

87

turned around somehow in Hawthorne Crescent, and roared up in back of him.

"Where is she?" Ahern demanded, all sick-white again. "Where did she go, Richie? Are you sure you saw her? Are you positive?"

But McCallister only nodded silently, words being a little beyond him here.

"Then get in," Ahern shouted through the car window, the significant thing now — the overpowering thing, really — being that each of them knew Sheridan well, and that in each of them the other saw his first troubled concern mirrored and then immediately intensified. "Get in here, Richie! We'll use the car."

By this time, however, McCallister was incapable of logical thought. He ran on into the oval, saw three men leaving the tavern on the far side from him, started for them — and then understood that there was no help there, since they could not possibly have seen Miss Stewart cross this intersection minutes ago. So where could they begin to look for her? McCallister asked himself. In what street could they — He groaned in his throat, because from his position near Hawthorne Crescent he could see that no less than eight of the development streets curved away at spaced intervals from Parkway Oval. He ran again, foolishly. Then Ahern raced up beside him, shouting at him and touching his siren. That sound screamed out and away past all the sleeping rooftops in Parkway Heights; it also shocked McCallister's brain back to some semblance of reality. He swung onto the car, Ahern slowing for just a moment. The paper seller, raising his head quickly when he heard the siren, looked around at them.

In Sheridan's place, where he was sheltered in front by the billboard, and on one side by the blunt end of a row of single garages, he had been waiting for some time now with his blue overcoat buttoned up in a neat and careful manner across his white scarf. He kept his hands in his pockets, his head low, and in that position was no more than a shadow among other shadows under the billboard, with nothing of him distinguishable more than five feet away save the dim outline and attitude of the Homburg hat, still dapperly tilted. From a closer distance his face could be just glimpsed, but vaguely and without feature under the hatbrim, like a blur of reflected illumination, or lesser darkness. Weeds, high as his waist in some places, brushed gently though in an irregular line across the billboard supports; and over them Sheridan kept in view, minute after minute, that portion of Eckington Street leading westward to Parkway Heights.

Back of him, and over near the line of garages, half a dozen worn out old automobile tires glimmered from intense blackness with an effect like bleached rot. Wind rustled back there in soft whispers, twisting in puffs lighter than tumbleweed around swampy hollows, and then on into a wasteland pockmarked by the empty sores of dirt and neglect. On his left, and soaring with abrupt magnificence above all this area, Parkway Heights had the magical appearance of some detached and independent city, all shining pale stone, with each roof crowned by the square masonry hut of its elevator housing, and the stairway windows lit all the way up, building after building, in a straight line. Now and again Sheridan would turn his gaze to these structures with a kind of tensely agitated composure, the Homburg graceful as ever to one side of his head, the gray eyes tightened across the surface but watchful and wide open, perhaps strained a bit also, with the whites very clear and prominent. It was cold in here, a sharp, clear night with the wind as yet no more than playfully active; and a remote low hum, the beehive activity of a city never wholly at ease and quiet, had begun now to distract and annoy him to some extent under the billboard.

He felt neither so patient nor so unmoved as he had expected to feel in these circumstances. Had she got a cab? Had someone given her a lift? Had Ahern seen her, and questioned her? It was impossible to decide on the right answer, if any was right; all he could do was to attempt to time her mentally. A few minutes to dress; then the elevator; then the hunt for a taxicab; then the start over here on foot. Only one street to use, Sheridan assured himself, and that the one he was on now. Another minute or two, perhaps; but then, surely . . . His billy he kept in the side pocket of his overcoat; and he would twist his fingers around the handle every so often, tighten them, change their position slightly, change again, and at last clamp down on the weapon with a slippery hand pressure before starting the whole business over again.

What was keeping her?

He did not know; he soon found himself unable even to guess whether it had been five minutes, or ten, or fifteen, since he had made his telephone call. He moved a couple of steps one way, then the other; but he still saw no one out there in the street, and heard no one.

What was keeping her?

He became nervous and irritable. For a good part of his adult life he had dealt with people who contrived situations of this kind under roughly analogous conditions; and he had come to regard with a characteristic Sheridan contempt the hesitations, the clumsiness of mind and the psychic blocks and handicaps which betrayed them nine times out of ten to men like Frank Eckstrom. He had never expected to find such emotional difficulties in himself; yet they were present. And not just a single worry or nagging impulse, which he would have been able to cancel out or ignore after the necessary effort; but a seething mixture of them — increasing uncertainty as to what was happening elsewhere with Ahern and McCallister (Frank Eckstrom also), fear as to his own safety in what he had decided to do here, doubt and worry for the way Miss Stewart would act — or had acted by now — after his phone call. He had not allowed in anticipation for the existence in him of any of these disturbing elements; but at this point, when he tried to dismiss one of them, all the rest

91

drove at him with a united and accumulating effect of jumpy nervousness.

What was keeping her?

He did two or three foolish things. He lit a cigarette before catching himself; then he allowed a bit of paper rustling around by his feet to upset him so much that he had to kneel anxiously with less than his usual quick grace, snatch it and crumple it; then a car passed on Eckington Street and he found himself crouching away from it with one knee in the mud and the fingers of the same hand balancing him.

He was furious with himself then, knowing that movement of any kind was the one thing that invariably caught the eyes. What was the matter with him, anyway? Why was he doing all the wrong things, knowing better and yet not able to act better? His lips compressed, and then set themselves; but he could not work free from an idea that this action which had seemed so simple and uncomplicated in outline a short time ago had now become dangerously clouded over by a hundred unforeseen risks and uncertainties.

He began thinking of that nurse as of someone who had done him an inexcusable personal injury. It helped. Then he thought up what appeared to be appropriate names for her. They helped also. In his thoughts now it was she who had become responsible for all this, since of course everything would have gone off perfectly, just as was planned, if she had not seen him coming out of the Wheeler apartment. He knew he could have handled

Ahern for the rest of it — managed him, broken him; and then in the morning, with the convertible safe and waiting on Narcissus Road . . .

He raised his head suddenly; he had heard something. He put his left side to the street, his extended arm parting the weeds carefully, the Homburg hat and the agitated white face under it incongruous both with each other and in that setting of squalor and shadow. He held his breath for a moment; but after that it was exactly the way he had wanted it. He had known at once that the footsteps he heard were a girl's footsteps, and he saw now that the girl coming along, pausing under the corner street lamp down from him as if she had run herself out of breath, was McCallister's little friend from apartment 8A.

She looked back at the development as if still hoping for a taxicab from it, and then came on towards him at a fast walk but on the other side of the street. Now, Sheridan told himself, when she had drawn even with him, and started to pass him. Now! But nothing at all happened; he stayed where he was as if his muscular responses had refused to obey him. Would he be seen now from perhaps blocks away slipping out after her — caught, chased, held? He had to fight that suggestion suddenly, as if what he wanted to do now, really wanted, was to stay safe where he was in the darkness and security back of his billboard. It was not that any compunction in regard to the girl moved him; if he could have had her dead and destroyed there by raising a finger he

93

would have done so with no feeling other than one of overwhelming relief. But to realize that there was only one way out for him now, that he had to quiet this girl, and that he had to do it himself . . .

He remained motionless for perhaps ten seconds. How could he be sure that there was nobody near — perhaps a couple murmuring in a parked car, or a man on his way home from the subway to Parkway Heights (When had the last train come in there? Couldn't he remember?), or a uniformed cop stealing a cigarette for himself in some isolated doorway chosen so that he could see his sergeant long before the sergeant would have a chance to see him? But of course in all these possibilities there lay no prospect of safety for him, only the reverse, rather, of absolute failure now through irresolute inaction; and in the end it was only the breakaway from those thoughts, the first step or two through the weeds, that presented any difficulty at all. As soon as they had been taken he was in complete control of himself, and became in mind and action quick, savage and resolved.

There was no one to be seen in the street but Miss Stewart. She looked back, hearing him, just as he cut across at her from his position, running lightly on his toes, and with the idea in him to head her off in the darkest section of the block, between the corner of a wooden fence and another billboard. This gave her a chance to run a few steps, or to scream — but she did not react to it with the necessary quickness. She watched him, not sure yet, perhaps; then she was foolish enough to back

94

away into the fence, attempting at the last moment to thrust her handbag into Sheridan's possession.

"Take it!" she breathed. "Please take it! I won't try to — "

But then Sheridan had her cornered. He went in low, forgetting the billy, forgetting everything but that a girl like this would have very little physical strength to fight against him. He ducked away from the handbag, came up beside her, locked his right arm around her throat and then swung her up and around into his chest. She was a very small girl. She dropped the pocketbook, tearing with both hands at Sheridan's overcoat sleeve; but by now, of course, she was unable to make any kind of audible sound.

There seemed to be a great tumult inside Sheridan's head, however — a vast whining and screaming. Not from her, obviously. She could gag, that was all; then her toes began to strike with insane lightness and rapidity against the pavement. Something else happened. The noise was not just in Sheridan's head any more; it was all around them, a piercing, animal-like scream rising and falling. It raced over from the development, higher and closer to him at each instant, and more shrilly penetrating with its effect of maddened and yet somehow imploring urgency. Sheridan, who had heard it often before from the good end, the safe end, at last placed it for what it was — a police siren. He dropped Miss Stewart. He ran three or four steps.

Finish the job! he thought then. That wasn't for him —

95

couldn't be! Get her in off the street, out of sight; and then even if the squad car roared by here — He ran back, yanking the billy out of his overcoat pocket and letting it slip away from him in his haste and clumsiness. On her hands and knees, sobbing for breath, Miss Stewart did all she could: she threw the handbag at him. Then powerful headlights raced up under the railroad trestle and glared at Sheridan across the road; and the department car, screaming way over onto the wrong lane, was yanked around crazily from the back end when Ahern tried to brake it into the curb beside them.

Several things happened so quickly that they were all parts of the one thing. A voice shouted at him; somebody else, without any kind of warning, fired at him across the top of the car. He turned his head wildly and saw McCallister out on the road, staggering from momentum, while the car swung around and away from him. Sheridan ran, and McCallister had to dance and sidestep breathlessly to regain balance. The headlights picked Sheridan up by the board fence — scrambling there, frantic; and behind him McCallister flopped to one knee, his left arm all the way out to poise himself, but his right arm straight ahead and emptying the big service revolver at Sheridan, blast after blast.

He missed. Ahern jumped out over the girl, the car door banging around after him.

"Over there by the fence!" McCallister bawled, already sprinting ahead from the road and digging hurriedly at his belt for the ammunition. "Get up to the corner, Paddy — then work down! I'll take it from here."

There was time to give that girl no more than a glance and a few words. "Stay by the car!" McCallister shouted at her. "Don't move from it! Do you hear me?" He must have been heard over on Broadway. Then he reached the fence, running so fast on his jack-rabbit legs that he fell or slipped around the upper end of it.

Sheridan had vanished.

Before McCallister there extended a blackness like inky water at the bottom of a clear lake, no details visible in it at any point but the fire Sheridan had seen earlier glimmering very low over by the railroad embankment. "Paddy!" McCallister roared. Ahern answered him from the upper end of the lot, and McCallister raced immediately in that direction, knowing that their only chance now was to pin Sheridan between them, and to drive him ahead of them towards the street lights.

His lungs hurt, his knees where he had fallen and scraped them, his ankle where he had twisted it in jumping clear of the car seconds ago. But these things were nothing, because the helpless and insane rage in him at what he had seen of little Miss Stewart back there on the sidewalk was the real torment. He was sure now what Sheridan would be prepared to do to him just as quickly and savagely as he was prepared to do it to Sheridan; yet the knowledge lent him no kind of caution. He ran on blindly towards Ahern — stopped once, listened, and tried to detect Sheridan against the undefended north and east side of the field.

But after that he understood that it was almost hopeless; the area in here, the uneven ground, the deep shadows, would have made it difficult for two men to trap a third even in light dusk. Gone, McCallister told himself. He had needed a start of only a few seconds; and now he had got them.

He stopped where he was, and Ahern thrashed up — big, clumsy, a face like death on him.

"Did you see him?" Ahern said. "Did you hear him anywhere, Richie?"

They stood together, listening. All they caught was another siren way over on Broadway. The lots stretched around them with no visible movement nearby, no disturbance of any kind; while over on the railroad embankment a string of freight cars rumbled along with the caboose window and a red lamp winking away from them on the long outward curve around Parkway Heights. Behind was the board fence, outlined dimly, above and below, by the street illumination; west lay the development, floating serene above all this like a city of the year after tomorrow. Over the lots was cold and bitter December starlight, and around them nothing more than the wind hunting and whispering at uneasy shadows.

"If I'd known what he was up to," Ahern said, the piglike small eyes wearily contracting themselves. "If I'd guessed, Richie — "

"If you'd known!" McCallister snarled at him, not quite normal yet after the wire-tight tension of these past few minutes. "If you'd guessed! What the hell do you need to figure him out after something like this?" His voice rose passionately. "Don't you see what he wanted to do — what he started to do? I'll tell you this much: I wouldn't have grabbed him in here if I had the chance to grab him. I'd have killed him. I come in here to kill him."

And that statement he meant quite literally at the moment. All the way over here from the development there had been the paralyzing dread in him that perhaps they would be too late to do anything effective for that girl; that already, because of Ahern's slowness in mentioning her, Sheridan might have been given the chance to complete his part of the job. It was not an emotion which McCallister found himself able to throw off immediately; the bare recollection of it, he clinging erect on the doorstep of the car, the night air slashing and tearing at him across the roof, and nothing to see — nothing to see! — for two blocks along that desolate street but emptiness and shadow, was intolerable to him.

"And who has she got to thank?" he demanded ferociously, turning on the other man now because he was unable to turn on Sheridan. "You or that paper seller who was able to tell us what street she took ? Or maybe you wanted it like this. Maybe you thought you wouldn't have anything to worry about with her gone. Sure! Sheridan did it! Sheridan did it!" He became shrill, aping Ahern in falsetto. "You're beginning to make me ashamed I ever knew you. Why did you bother to open your mouth about that kid? Why didn't you just go ahead and let Sheridan take care of her?"

"Please, Richie!" Ahern said. He turned his head from McCallister and fumbled at the right side of his mouth, the fingers digging in there, but all shaking, and extended clawlike. "You know I never thought he'd do this. So don't — " But he made no other attempt to defend himself; he never did with McCallister. He just kept his head away and his ugly little eyes hidden, looking inward perhaps at the misery and hopelessness of his own heart.

"A guy I worked with!" McCallister raged at him. "A guy I looked out for time after time because he never had the guts or sense to look out for himself! And then what were you ready to do to protect a louse like Sheridan? What did that girl out there mean to you? Nothing!"

He was still distraught because of the razor-sharp distinction between getting to Miss Stewart in time, and not getting to her at all. Because of this he made a menacing gesture with one fist towards Ahern — almost struck him.

"Get away from me!" he said. "Get out of my sight! Or go out and find him. I guess you know where to look. That's probably another thing you had all fixed up between you."

Ahern's mouth turned ash gray.

"You don't mean that," he said. "You can't, Richie."

"Can't I?" McCallister said, savage there also. "You know that, do you? All right, then. I guess you want to come back with me and talk to that girl. Come on! I'll let you explain to her. I'll let you say how and why — "

He started off.

"Wait a minute," Ahern said, fumbling after him. "Don't leave me alone. Don't turn on me, Richie. Then who would I have? Who else — "

"Who did you pick?" McCallister asked him, again knocking his hand away. "Me or Sheridan? No, don't come near me. I can't even talk to you any more. I can't stand the sight of you."

He left Ahern there. He ran back to the fence, and found Miss Stewart huddled up in the front seat of the car with the headlights still on and the front door hanging open. She gave him a forward inclination of the head, jerkily; but beyond that one sign of recognition there seemed to be nothing at all in her but a frozen aftereffect of shock, sickness and physical terror. She had her arm up on the back of the seat, and now she laid the side of her face against it, staring into the lots back of McCallister — into a darkness greater than any she had ever had to consider before.

"Did he hurt you?" McCallister demanded harshly, the strange and difficult thing for him to remember being that the bond between them, built up night after night in the living room at 8E with McCallister at one end of the binoculars and she at the other, was all on his part and none on hers.

Not even her eyelids blinked.

"What did he want?" she whispered up at him. "I tried

101

to give him my pocketbook, but he wouldn't take it. Why did he — "

"The Lieutenant will tell you," McCallister said, gulping some breath into him. "I can't. Don't ask me."

"The Lieutenant?" she asked unsteadily. "What lieutenant?"

So McCallister had to give her a few words explaining himself, and the night watch at 1775 Hawthorne Crescent. She might have recognized that man, he added, his teeth gritting together; he was the same one she had seen a couple of hours ago in the apartment right next to her.

"You mean he wanted to kill me," she said, putting out a hand blindly at him, so that he took it and pressed it hard between both of his. "That's why he got me down here. There wasn't an accident at all with Molly. He just — "

"Don't think about it," McCallister advised her, looking back towards the lot for Paddy Ahern. "We'll get him. Not tonight, maybe; but as soon — "

Then the other police car, the one he had heard earlier, raced up from Broadway, and he had to identify himself to the two uniformed men in it. They ran back of the billboards afterward, fanning out to where he had left Ahern with their flashlights darting and circling in front of them.

"You saw something," McCallister informed her, "that you didn't know. But you could have identified him for the Lieutenant tomorrow; and then he'd have had to

102

explain a lot of things. He had it thought out, all right. You didn't. How could you?"

She shivered. She looked up at McCallister, her breath caught, and she began to weep quietly. There wasn't much that McCallister could do then but leave her alone, no matter how he felt; so he got her into the back of the car, and joined a patrolman who had come running up from the development. Where was Paddy? he began asking himself. He remembered a few of the things he had said to Ahern in that passionate outburst; he flushed. But of course Paddy would never have taken him at face value. Because he knew — He ran up onto a rise of ground, looking around from there. "Paddy!" he roared powerfully.

There was no answer.

Eckstrom arrived in the black coupé, having picked up a little of this commotion on his car radio; and of course Eckstrom had to be told everything then from the moment of Ahern's confession. Twice, considering his narration ended, McCallister started back for the lots; and twice, laying a thick paw on his wrist, Eckstrom yanked him back apparently without effort.

"You didn't tell me about that car," Eckstrom accused him. "Who has the keys to it? Sheridan?"

"I don't know," McCallister said, pulling away again. "We didn't talk any about that part. Now let me look for him, will you? He's out there somewhere."

The uniformed men were beginning to show up again, one by one. No Ahern, though.

103

"He'll take his chance," Eckstrom declared grimly. "Better men do. I'm asking you if you think Sheridan has the keys to that car. If he does, wouldn't you say he'd head for it after this, and for the money?"

McCallister, pausing after a couple of fast steps, turned very slowly towards him.

"What else?" Eckstrom said, smacking his big palms together. "For the love of heaven, McCallister! Where did they leave it?"

But it took McCallister a long moment to recall the information. He was thinking of Ahern heading over for Narcissus Road with no help — doing what he had been directed so scornfully to do, starting out to find Sheridan. And he had never been any good with the gun, McCallister remembered. Say he got to Narcissus Road in time; say he found Sheridan there; and say he tried to stop Sheridan. Then . . .

"Will you tell me what I'm asking you?" Eckstrom barked, short and savage with him now. "Where's that car?"

"Behind the crescent," McCallister husked at him. "A couple of blocks in on that new street they haven't finished yet. Narcissus Road."

"Then let's get over there," Eckstrom said. "Fast. And let's block it off between us from the two ends."

They all broke for the cars — McCallister, the three uniformed men, Frank Eckstrom. "What is it?" Miss Stewart asked the moment she saw McCallister's face. "Now what's happened?"

104

But he was hardly conscious of her in the seat behind him. I didn't mean it, he was thinking desperately. Wait for me now, Paddy! Wait for me!

Ahern, however, had acquired a considerable start on all of them by that time. He had watched McCallister run back towards the street after their conversation; he had felt absolutely nothing inside him; and then he became aware that his fingers had groped for a leather key ring in his overcoat pocket, and stopped on it as if to impress him with the significance of what might have been their own independent action. He took it out and glanced at it dully. Wheeler's, he remembered. He started to put it back. He stopped, looking down at it. Suddenly, through simple association, the key ring made him think of the convertible; the convertible of the money; and the money, at once and with absolute certainty, of the one place now where he might have a chance of locating Walter Sheridan.

At once he began to run in a clumsy and pounding fashion, heading away from the fence and the department car, and west toward the railroad embankment. The girl back there had not the private and personal importance for him which she had for McCallister; yet he could think only with crawling horror of what Sheridan had attempted to do to her. Finish it with him now! was Ahern's thought. Why not? Hadn't he begun it with him? Mixed with this was another idea: that it was imperative for him to approach Narcissus Road by himself, with no reinforcements, if he was to have any chance of decoying Sheridan out into the open. With McCallister present, or a couple of uniformed men, Sheridan would never show himself; but if he spotted Ahern alone back there, and if he believed, as he should, that they were still bound to each other by mutual interest . . .

The idea made itself perfectly clear in Ahern's mind as he ran on into the lots, stumbling once or twice on the bad footing and soon having to pant hoarsely as he labored himself forward. He scrambled up over the railroad embankment, driven ahead by the hot shame in him when he thought of that girl, and of what, even as an unwitting accomplice, Sheridan had very nearly made of him. It could not have been more than two minutes after McCallister left him when he plunged out into the upper end of Narcissus Road, saw the convertible and wobbled on towards it with his thigh muscles jumping and quivering under him like jelly — from the physical exertion, however, and not from any remaining fear or uncertainty in his thoughts. He knew Richie had been right; he knew Richie was always right. And that meant he had to stop Sheridan here — his last chance; because if he did not — He paused beside the convertible. "Walter!" he called softly. "Walter!"

He carried the gun a little back of him so that Sheridan would not see it at once. But there was no need. There was no Sheridan. He wiped his mouth, pocketed the revolver; then he got into the convertible and drove it back down the hill toward Hawthorne Crescent, parking it there in an empty place just up from 1775. Now, when Richie and Eckstrom arrived, they would find at least these things waiting for them — the car, the dead man, the money and Paddy Ahern. It was almost enough; Sheridan would complete it. Had he, perhaps, taken a safer and so more circuitous route back to the convertible? And could he be up on Narcissus Road now watching and waiting to contact Ahern without anyone else around?

It did not seem very probable; but still Ahern went back to the corner of Narcissus Road, hesitated there, and walked up the center of the street. There was no Sheridan, of course, not even when he had reached the end of the second block in, and stopped there. He grinned wearily. Perhaps there was always a trick to it, he thought; perhaps, in the end, redemption was never quite so simple. "Walter!" he called again, but not really expecting to see Sheridan this time. "Walter!"

Then he started back. He felt that he understood himself with a penetration deeper and truer than any he had been vouchsafed before; and because of this he tried to decide in his thoughts if qualities like courage and integrity were free gifts, or if perhaps everyone had to work for them slowly and patiently, building them up little by little, nourishing them, and watching out for them. That might be so, Ahern thought; what fooled you was that they were never important when you did not need them. But when you did . . .

107

Out of an unfinished apartment doorway across from where the convertible had been parked a few minutes ago there came a sharp hiss, and then an arm and hand half glimpsed and beckoning to him urgently. He stopped, putting his hand into his overcoat pocket for the revolver. He saw the Homburg hat and the face under it turning quickly from one end of this avenue to the other; then Walter Sheridan darted across to him, and they met again, for the last time, and now from much different motives, under the protection of that sidewalk roof on Narcissus Road where everything had started a little more than three hours ago.

PART FOUR

"WHERE'S THE CAR?" Sheridan demanded at once. "And where's McCallister? We're in kind of a jam, Paddy, and we got to get out of here as quick as we can — because I caught him talking to that girl five or ten minutes ago. I know she's gonna tell him about me — about us. That's why I've been looking for you. So where did you put the car? Why did you move it?"

Even after what had just happened, Ahern realized, he was not going to be told the truth about this; he would be lied to again — used, fooled, discarded — because apparently there had been no time for Sheridan to recognize him back on Eckington Street.

"You'd better stop it," he said. "It's no good any more. I know what you did — how you lied to me about going upstairs. I saw you back there. I was driving Richie."

There was a rapid inward flicker across Sheridan's gray eyes.

"Then you're the one told him about that girl! It was you! You were in back of the whole thing!"

"That's right," Ahern nodded quietly. "I told him

109

everything we did up here — everything. And that's why he wanted to kill you for what you tried on Eckington Street. I ought to."

He had taken the revolver out of his pocket, and Sheridan looked at it, and then up at him. Immediately after this he did an unexpected and reckless thing: he walked over to Ahern and slapped him across the mouth. Use the whip, he told himself. It had worked before. It would have to work now.

"Who do you think you're pointing that at?" he demanded savagely. "So now you'll bring me in with the gun on me, will you? Like hell! You're going to tell me what you did with that car, and give me the keys to it. I'm getting out of here. There's nobody going to put Walter Sheridan away in a stinking and dirty hole for the rest of his life. Nobody!"

Ahern wiped his mouth very calmly.

"No. You're coming back with me, Walter."

"Am I?" Sheridan said, even more softly. But he seemed aware of the gun now; he would start to look at it, stop, and then dart the gray eyes back to Ahern's face. His own was blood-dark. "Then maybe I did the whole thing myself," he said. "Sure! That's the sweet little angle Richie McCallister cooked up for you. You take me in with the gun on me, and then I'm the one — " He yanked loose the white scarf around his throat, as if it had begun choking him. "That's the idea, isn't it? But you ain't out of it yet. You rotten, sneaking bastard! I'll say you got me to kill Wheeler deliberately, like I did, and like you know I did. I'll swear to Christ that it was you talked me into — "

"So we get the truth now," Ahern said, narrowing his eyes tiredly. "What you really did it for. Not for me. For that money."

"And they're gonna know about the girl, too," Sheridan breathed, his eyes blazing darkly at Ahern from under thin blond brows. "They'll get me for that, even! And I had to try it — I had to! — because if I'd told you about it you'd just have run squealing to McCallister. The way you did anyway!"

"You ought to get down on your knees," Ahern told him, his voice shaking a little, but not for the reason it would have shaken a couple of hours ago during a conversation of this kind, "because we were in time to stop you on that. You ought to thank God you didn't do any harm to her. I mean it, Walter!" He made a sudden and imploring gesture at Sheridan with the revolver. "It's just been spreading out and out on us all the time. First Wheeler; then that girl; then Eckington Street. I don't think you know what you're doing any more! It's like you're — "

Something must have happened to him, Sheridan realized dumbly. He intended to do what he said; he actually — Without any further reflection, from instinct at the reckless and sidewise manner in which Ahern had extended the revolver to him, he lunged for it.

"Walter!" Ahern cried. "Don't make me use it. No, Walter!"

111

He had time to fire at least once at Sheridan; he did not. He just attempted to keep the gun from him, and they staggered around fighting for it. Sheridan breathed out gutter names. He got both hands on the gun, Ahern pulled it away, or tried to, and there were a couple of reports muffled between them. Again the bigger but clumsier man tried to grab at him, and Sheridan reeled off in a continuation of the fierce bodily wrench that had torn him clear of Ahern, and at the same moment discharged the service revolver almost against him.

"You did it!" Sheridan panted. "You shot me!"

He stumbled. He went down onto his right knee whimpering and clawing at himself; all the stories he had heard of men being shot as the climax of a struggle, and for a moment, with all the excitement, not feeling anything at all, darted through his mind and convinced him of a mortal wound somewhere. He dropped the gun and began to breathe in anxious and pitiable gasps, no pain yet, but still unable to believe that at such close quarters neither of the shots had taken effect on him. Ahern, still standing erect, lurched at him.

"Damn you!" Sheridan sobbed. "Damn you!"

Then Ahern collapsed over him. He had received both bullets upward through the side of the head.

"What is it?" Sheridan whispered, now in his own overpowering relief frantic to have Ahern safe and unharmed also. "What's wrong with you? I didn't want this! Listen to me! You're not hurt, are you? Paddy!"

But it was obvious at once that Ahern, who had rolled

112

over into the sandpile with his head and shoulders arching up and back and his mouth gagging open, had been terribly wounded. A metallic rattle began in his throat; he moaned hoarsely; his head rolled back towards Sheridan and the whites of his eyes could be seen glaring and swollen low under the lids like thick gelatin. He was not conscious. For a moment Sheridan crouched forward on his knees, staring down at him with an obscure personal fascination of loathing and revulsion. The noise in Ahern's throat changed back to the first rattle, rose, stopped halfway up on an inhalation and choked liquidly. Sheridan jumped up. The only intelligent thought he had was not concerned with Ahern. All alone now, Sheridan told himself. All alone.

Twice he started for Ahern, and each time stopped himself, wanting to assist somehow, wanting desperately to bring Ahern back; but all this, primarily, for his own sake and not for Ahern's. For a short while he stood motionless against the wooden construction fence with Ahern at his feet and a kind of thunderous pounding inside his ears, as if he had been placed suddenly in the heart of a silent but ringing vacuum. He backed off a couple of more steps, without the least idea of where to go now, or what to do. He was badly confused, making a false start in one direction from Ahern before remembering the convertible keys and running back for them. They were in Ahern's overcoat pocket. He snatched them out, started to run again, slipped and jumped up breathlessly; and then before he had raced halfway to

113

the upper corner of Narcissus Road a black coupé rolled around from the cross street and swung in at him.

He recognized it at once as Frank Eckstrom's. Well concealed as he was by the darkness under the sidewalk roof, by cement troughs and contractors' equipment lined up here against the curbing, he did not think to crouch in that position — to let Eckstrom's car pass him and then go on in the direction he had chosen, which he could have done very easily. The panic had mastered him. He ran back. He had nearly reached the spot where he had left Ahern when McCallister and the other department car turned in at him from the direction of Hawthorne Crescent.

He threw himself into the plank fence, smashing against it with both shoulders, then came out from it and again slipped in trying to start too fast from the complete stop. There was a door beside him. He caught sight of it in getting up, yanked at the knob, stumbled through and then swung it shut after him. Resting against it, hearing the cars just outside, coming together there, he still had to stand motionless for another instant while long shudders passed all the way up and out through his body. He had wanted Ahern dead; he had thought how fine it would make everything if Ahern killed himself; but now, even in his panic-stricken reaction to the arrival of McCallister and Frank Eckstrom, he was beginning to see that Ahern had been the one aide and confidant left to him. And all this time, of

114

course, he had to endure from the other side of the fence Ahern's labored and agonizing struggle for breath.

A car door opened and slammed, then another. He put his hands back against the door, on either side of him, and glared around hurriedly. What held him was a long, narrow space shut off from the street by the construction fence, and in front by the unfinished wall of a new apartment building. Two planks led up over a shallow areaway to the front door, but there were other boards crisscrossed over this opening and so barring it as a means of exit. Again Sheridan whimpered deep in his throat. Now Ahern was well out of it, as he had wanted to be. But Walter Sheridan? On the other side of the fence, so close to him that he ducked down with a terrified and yet savage contraction of the mouth, he heard Eckstrom muttering toughly at someone:

" — busy on it, and look around. No, the second block in is all I can tell you; that's the way he described it to McCallister. Spread out now, and watch yourselves. They're around here someplace, the two of them."

There was much hurried and confused movement, a scuffle and stop near the sandpile, a man's voice crying out in surprise there.

"What?" Eckstrom demanded sharply. "What is it?"

"Over this way," the voice said. "There's somebody lying here, Lieutenant. Jesus! It looks like Ahern to me."

Eckstrom made hurried but solid steps on the plank walk. There was a dead pause. Someone ran up from the other car, from McCallister's car.

"Leave him alone," Eckstrom said, the obvious sick helplessness in his voice showing that he had seen Ahern's wound, and felt the usual layman's dread of doing the wrong thing for it. "I don't want him touched by anyone until we get a doctor up here. McCallister!"

But McCallister, who had stopped short out there and then uttered one heartbroken, keening cry, must not have paid any attention to him.

"Damn it! Will you not lift him?" Eckstrom swore passionately. "Will you listen to me?"

"Come on," somebody else said. "Come on, Richie. You don't know what you might do to him."

"Here, let me," little Miss Stewart said, her voice wavering the least bit. "I'll hold him. I'm afraid he's choking himself that way."

It became possible to hear Ahern again — the rattle, the sustained breathless gasp, the stop; this sequence repeated over and over. The tremendous physical effort of it seemed to be in Sheridan's chest also, so that, unable to endure it without reaction, he put his fist to his mouth and from above it stared blindly into the areaway.

"What the hell are you all standing around for?" Eckstrom demanded then. "There's a doctor on Hawthorne Crescent, isn't there? Run down and get him, one of you — and get the priest while you're at it. Mahoney!" Mahoney ran off, clattering on the plank walk. "Is he conscious?" Eckstrom said. "Do you think you could talk to him?"

"Can you hear me, Paddy?" McCallister begged. "Can you understand me?"

"Lieutenant," another voice said. "What kind of a car was it? Shouldn't we try to — "

"We don't know," Eckstrom declared heavily. "We just don't know. He never told McCallister."

"Tire marks," Eckstrom's driver yelled at him, very much excited by that discovery. "In the sand here, Lieutenant. Look."

"See if he's got any keys on him," Eckstrom said. There was more hurried movement. "No," somebody said. "Just his own." Eckstrom's voice flattened out. "Then Sheridan took the car with him," he said. "Of course. It was the quickest and safest way out of here."

Out of here? Sheridan thought. He looked around over the clenched fist, his eyes gliding back without any corresponding movement of the head.

"See if you can get him to nod," Eckstrom directed. "To blink his eyes at you, McCallister. To do anything."

"Paddy," McCallister said, speaking with a soft, rapid blur over his words. "We're going to get you fixed up, Paddy; don't worry about it; but now the Lieutenant wants to know something about that car. You know Richie, don't you? And you can try to — " His voice broke altogether. "Look at him!" he breathed at Eckstrom. "Listen to him!"

"All right," Eckstrom said, conceding it then. He came back toward Sheridan; his voice dropped a bit, perhaps to leave McCallister out of this, but remained grimly audible near the construction fence. "And that's Mr. Sheridan's work for tonight," he said. "Or part of it. Our Mr. Sheridan. Who's driving that squad car?"

He gave orders. The squad car was sent off to make a quick tour of the adjacent streets, to watch for Sheridan or anything suspicious, and then to report back; his own driver, after this, was instructed to go down to the Wheeler apartment at 1775 Hawthorne Crescent.

"Talk to the wife," Eckstrom said, "and find out if she can tell us anything about that automobile. We need that right away; and we need it bad. Tell her about the husband first thing; slap her in the face with it the minute she opens the door for you; and then call Healey downtown if she can give you a description of it. If she can't, or if she tells you she can't, stay in the room with her, and keep your mouth shut; but don't let her call anybody, or slip out of the apartment on you. I'll handle it then. I'll be down there the minute this thing is over."

Another of the cars started away; Eckstrom went over again towards McCallister. "I think he's better," McCallister said, now breathlessly insistent. "He looks better — a lot better, Lieutenant. Doesn't he?"

"The man's dying before your eyes," Eckstrom said. "Where's that doctor?"

In back of the fence Sheridan breathed very quietly. Get out of here now, he warned himself; and get out while they were all watching Ahern. He knelt beside the areaway, letting himself down into it with great caution.

118

He watched the fence while dropping into the areaway from it; at the bottom, after his shoe scraped into some rubble, he froze against the wall, looking up then with his revolver ready and his mouth twisted back on him.

He felt better, because now he had no longer to listen to Paddy Ahern; he felt more like Sheridan again. Had me, he thought, exulting nervously over all of them; had me right in their hands; and missed me. The great Frank Eckstrom! An open cellarway led him on under the building; he groped ahead in there feeling himself more secure after every careful step forward. In his mind was the almost incredulous knowledge that they knew nothing at all about the car, and had no suspicion that it was Ahern, and not he, who had driven it away from Narcissus Road. Could he still find it before they did, and get the money? Why not? He was prepared to recognize it at sight, and from blocks distant; they could walk by it, unless they got a description somewhere, without so much as a second glance.

Hope and excitement stirred him. What was his position without the money, with just the few dollars he had in his pockets now? No position at all, Sheridan knew. Because his family and friends would be watched from now on, as Mrs. Wheeler had been watched, and Sheridan himself cut off in that way from whatever assistance or shelter they might have been tempted to give to him. He must never make the mistake that Wheeler had made; beginning right now, he must never attempt to get in touch with anyone who had known him. What then?

119

On his person he had perhaps fourteen or fifteen dollars; but in that convertible . . .

Two or three buildings away, at the foot of some stairs leading up to a back yard where there was only row upon row of blank windows to look down at him, he risked a badly needed cigarette, sheltering himself for it behind an array of uninstalled laundry machines. Ahern, he suspected, had not moved the car very far from its original position; the time element had been against it. He had moved it, of course, because he had not wanted Sheridan to find it unprotected, to smash open the trunk and get the money; but now, around here somewhere, it was still waiting for Sheridan, and only for Sheridan — unless and until Mrs. Wheeler could give them the information they needed about it.

But even then they were going to be far off the track. They believed now, from the tire marks and because the keys had not been found in Ahern's possession, that the car had been taken away; and so for the next few hours they would have neither the time, men nor inclination to make a street-by-street search for it through the development. They had too many other wheels to start turning. Tomorrow morning, if nothing worked itself out meanwhile, they would cover this neighborhood with care and thoroughness; but just now, and for the next hour or two, Eckstrom was going to be very much occupied with getting a hunt organized from up here by telephone.

Then suppose he waited them out? Sheridan thought.

Say he gave them an hour or two, until four, perhaps, to question Mrs. Wheeler, to confer together, and to do their telephoning from apartment 8E. What would they do after that? He was helped here by his familiarity with them. Leave for downtown, probably, after warning the beat patrolman and the district squad car to keep their eyes open for what Eckstrom must privately consider a very remote chance. And therefore by four o'clock, Sheridan decided, he should be able to slip out of here and start looking for that convertible with a comparatively free hand. So let them get started on the routine procedure; let them do whatever they wanted to do; and then let them catch a man who, from long and intimate association, would know what they were up to in many cases before they even thought of it themselves. Or let them try!

He could see only one uncertainty in all this. Would Mrs. Wheeler be able to describe the convertible for them? Take that chance, Sheridan urged himself, since even with a description they would believe that the car had been moved elsewhere; and of course without money, without friends, without help, he might as well turn himself in to Frank Eckstrom right now. Then the heart of the matter began to harass and perplex him. What had Ahern done with the green convertible? He began concentrating on that, his brows wrinkling together in anxious folds and his hands moving nervously across the front of his overcoat. If Ahern had confessed everything, this could mean only that Ahern would have

121

hidden the car from him, but not from them. So where —
He made a quick and abrupt upward movement of the
head, snarling to himself soundlessly. He had an intui-
tion as to where the convertible was now: in the one
street where he could not possibly show himself to look
for it. Right in front of that building on Hawthorne Crescent, he thought savagely. Of course! Where else?

About this time up on Narcissus Road a middle-aged
doctor wearing a hat and overcoat over vivid yellow pajamas finished a hurried preliminary examination of
Paddy Ahern. Squatting for a moment on toes and finger-
tips, lips pursed, he must have considered one or two
courses of action; but then he only addressed a few low
words to Miss Stewart, snapped his bag in on itself and
rose puffing, with a middle-aged grimace of muscular
discomfort. "We won't move him," he said, giving Mc-
Callister assurance of the well-trained professional kind,
but with no actual promise implied in it. "Not yet. Not
till the ambulance gets here. And take it easy until then,
boy. Don't worry him."

McCallister reacted with several hurried nods.

"Sure," he said. "We'll wait till — "

"Maybe you'd better watch for it," Eckstrom suggested quietly. "Go on now, McCallister. Do as you're
told."

But after that there seemed to be an endless wait for
the ambulance. Several times McCallister darted into
the road looking for it, and feeling harried by the idea

122

that there was something he had to do here, but had forgotten — something very important. I'm going to take care of you, he thought breathlessly; you know that, Paddy, don't you? Night wind ran low and chill over his ankles, he became aware of it, and stripped the overcoat from himself. This he spread on Ahern, with Miss Stewart helping him. Then out to the road again, while the doctor shook his head and shrugged slightly at some question from Frank Eckstrom.

McCallister pretended to himself that he had not seen this, and had no idea what they were talking about. His teeth chattered. He began to stride up and down the pavement, all his hope centered now on the ambulance. Headlights appeared down by the crescent; he ran out and beckoned them on eagerly, using both hands. Now! he thought. But in another moment his stomach twisted around in him like a wrung dishrag. It was not the ambulance at all. It was the priest with Mahoney. No! McCallister thought then. He wasn't going to let this happen to Paddy; not here and not yet. "Wait," he said, appealing desperately to the priest. "Don't go over there. You'd scare him, Father. You'd only — "

"Get hold of yourself," Mahoney said, gripping him hard under the right arm. "It's got to be done, Richie. You know he's going."

Eckstrom removed his hat, clasped his hands low under his waist and began to gaze somberly at the pavement; and beneath the protective roof, his head resting on a seat pad from one of the cars, Ahern's face could be

123

seen dimly with the flesh waxen and petulant around his mouth, and very darkly shadowed around his eyes. Little Miss Stewart had been tucking McCallister's overcoat in at his shoulders; now she wiped his lips gently.

The priest knelt beside them, Mahoney crossed himself, one of the uniformed men cleared his throat and shifted position nervously; yet, for another moment, this final act and submission remained incomprehensible to McCallister. "Get over there," Eckstrom muttered at him. "He'd want you, wouldn't he?" What? McCallister thought. Who? His teeth chattered again; then he also knelt on the other side from the priest, with his jaw muscles set hard, in small lumps, and looked down at Ahern with an intent and slightly rigid expression.

It was just about over. On both knees, with his black coat unbuttoned and the ends of the stole swinging in front of him, the priest murmured rapidly in a hushed whisper while anointing the forehead and lips of Ahern with his right thumb. "Doctor," Miss Stewart said. Then the doctor came over to them just as Ahern made his first and only movement — a slight, pushing gesture of the hand, aimless, or perhaps reaching for something.

McCallister took the hand, and held it. I'm here, he wanted to tell Ahern; right here, Paddy. But the words died in his throat, and after that there was nothing more to be said to Ahern — or be done, either, not even by McCallister. His struggle for breath became quieter and quieter, hesitated, began again on a low sigh, stopped

124

altogether; the priest bent forward with his hands clasped into his chest and prayed silently; and McCallister, without a word or a thought in him, knelt there and watched the last unmistakable dignity and apartness stamp themselves on Ahern's features.

"Okay," McCallister said then, although no one had spoken to him. "Yep." He made a short, smacking sound of that syllable and got up at once, dusting his knee with his right hand. "Poor old Paddy," one of the men murmured behind him. "Poor old Paddy!" McCallister said nothing to that; but afterward he would not look at Ahern at all. He went over to the department car, dusted his knee again, moistened his lips and kept his back to everyone on the pavement. He noticed, as if his mind had become fixed on these details to the exclusion of any other thought, that it had turned into a bitter cold night brilliant with stars, and that overhead, distantly, there was beginning a vast surge and bellow of wind. A minute or two passed in that sharpness of physical sense much like the most serene placidity of mind; then Eckstrom joined him, the hat on again, the hacked face tough and stolid as ever.

"I guess you know there was nothing to be done for him," Eckstrom said. "Not by anyone."

"As soon as I looked at him," McCallister nodded, his voice perfectly normal, but his eyes with a dry, hot shininess to them. "Of course. I just wouldn't admit it."

"Do you want to go over it again?" Eckstrom said. "About that car? Think of it for a minute, because we'll need the description. Can you remember anything that Ahern told you about it — anything at all?"

"What was in it," McCallister said. "Where it was." It had become difficult to manage his mouth properly; and so he pushed it out now and made a small o with it, as if trying to consider very carefully what Eckstrom had just asked him. "That's all. We were both — well, kind of upset. I'd been yelling at him; and I guess he thought I hated him in my heart. When all the time I knew he never wanted to get mixed up in this thing. Never."

"You can stand there," Eckstrom informed him with a kind of impatient and disgusted curtness, "and torment yourself about things no one can help any more; or you can let that go for a while, and try to do something to-night about Mr. Walter Sheridan. Now make up your mind, McCallister. Which is it?"

McCallister flushed.

"You didn't have to ask that," he said.

"Didn't I?" Eckstrom said. "I thought maybe I did. Get a drink now and come up to the Wheeler apartment after you've had it. I might have some use for you."

He went away. Miss Stewart hovered uncertainly near the back of the car, McCallister's overcoat on her arm; and behind her, projecting from something shapeless and covered over by a strip of contractors' canvas, could be seen Ahern's old-fashioned and knobby-toed black shoes, with each one resting on the outer side of the heel, and pointed away from the other in a Chaplin grotesque. McCallister's dark blue eyes began to shift around helplessly, wincing in, with an harassed effect of countless fine wrinkles, at each of the corners. Miss Stewart came over to him.

"Put on your overcoat," she said quietly. "It's cold And you're getting all chilled like this."

But he was altogether unaware of that now.

"I'll tell you what I did," he said, his mouth painfully re-forming around that small o. "I told him to keep away from me. 'Get out of here,' I said. 'Get out of my sight. You make me ashamed I ever knew you.' And that's what I got to remember now. That's the last thing that I ever said to him that he heard."

There seemed to be no adequate comment for her to make then.

"Put on your coat," she insisted gently. "Please."

And now at last the ambulance pulled into the curb beside them, its roof light winking and flashing. McCallister, buttoning himself up with stiff fingers, half turned back toward that heap of canvas, stopped himself, and started down the hill with her for Hawthorne Crescent. "And I went to hit him," he said, his features all muddy gray. "When he was trying to make up for everything. When he came over here to find Sheridan, and to stop him. That's what I did to someone who was as close to me — "

But of course Eckstrom had been a hundred per cent right about it; there was small point, and less comfort, in going over and over that last scene on the lots near Eckington Street. He went on silently, and in the vestibule at 1775 rang for the elevator, while Miss Stewart eyed him in a concerned and distressed way.

"Why don't you come upstairs for a minute?" she asked then, after the elevator door opened. "I'd make you some coffee."

"No, thanks," McCallister answered, with low effort. "I'd better — "

"But I want you to have it," she said, quiet and firm with him now. "So did the Lieutenant. I heard that. And it's no bother at all. I want some myself."

And that was how, at the rather odd hour of a quarter past two in the morning, McCallister entered at last a living room which he knew so well from the other side of the courtyard. She took his hat and his coat, and left him alone in there for a few moments while getting the coffee started out in the kitchen. He moved around. There were three books positioned to him on a table between elephant book ends, and he examined the title of each of them with much care. One was anatomy and physiology for nurses; the second a textbook on dietetics; and the third a detective story with the cover picture one of a dead man lying in front of a manorial English fireplace. Stabbed, McCallister noticed. He wondered if they had moved Paddy by now; or if he was still . . .

He swallowed a couple of times. He sat down and leaned back in a chair and closed his eyes for a while, listening to her move around quietly in the kitchen. Coffee began to bubble, and she appeared again to unfold a white cloth over a bridge table, and to set out the

128

coffee things on it. He watched her from under his lids — a slim, small girl in a brown dress, who'd had her own troubles tonight, but who still offered something warm, alive and very comforting just now against the memory of that sandpile back there on Narcissus Road.

"I used to watch you," he declared suddenly; anything here to get away from Ahern. "I used to sit over there in our apartment with some glasses we had, night after night. Just for something to do, I guess; or because — But you never knew about that, did you?"

"No, I didn't," Miss Stewart admitted, grave about it, quite serious. She had toast on, and had brought in the electric percolator. It smelt fine. "No idea, even."

"Well, that's what started it," McCallister told her, rubbing one hand over the new slip cover under him. "The way I got to know you. I saw you working on these, for instance — all last week; and I watched that party you gave tonight. You told them about me, didn't you?"

"I'm afraid I did," she confessed, coloring a bit. "But I never dreamed — Where were you, anyway? Just across there?"

He nodded to that; then he locked his fingers between his knees and bent the small head forward over them.

"I want to tell you about it," he explained huskily, "because I want you to understand how it happened tonight between me and Paddy. You weren't — " he hesitated, tried to find another term than the generic police one, and could not — "you weren't just another citizen to me; you were someone I knew pretty well, even before I

129

met you downstairs the other night. So when Paddy told me how you spotted Sheridan next door, I saw that it was going to be a snap of the fingers either way — whether we'd get to you in time, or whether we wouldn't. That's why I jumped all over him afterward. Because I'd got myself so worked up about Sheridan, and about you — "

His thoughts drifted back towards Narcissus Road, blurred in him, like shadowy streaks in deep water. "Crazy," he said, trying to shut his mind to that sand-pile. "Watching you like that night after night, and thinking — " He grinned painfully. "I guess I don't have good sense."

"Well," Miss Stewart said, giving no indication that she was either surprised or flustered by this news, "it was a — a special kind of experience, I suppose. But I hardly know what to — Here! Come on over and get your coffee."

He drank it, or part of it; he accepted a piece of buttered toast.

"Where's your friend?" he said. "You won't be here alone all night, will you?"

"I'm afraid so," she told him, her mouth going a little clumsy. "Molly's away until Monday. But that's all right. I'm not the kind — "

"Don't worry about him," McCallister said, looking up at her across the table with his blue eyes as hard and glittery as ocean ice. "You don't have to, because you're not important to him any more, not after Paddy. He's

130

running now, and he'll keep running. So I don't want you lying awake over here and getting upset about him. You won't, will you?"

"Oh no!" Miss Stewart whispered. But quite suddenly she had visualized Sheridan again, not by the lots, where she had failed even to recognize him, but as he had appeared in the doorway to the Wheeler apartment a few hours ago — the Homburg, the startled and then stony gray eyes under it, the good-looking bold features hating her, and desperately afraid of her, for a reason she had not understood then. Her hand shook holding the coffee cup; and McCallister pushed back from the bridge table, and stood up.

"I want you to get some rest," he said grimly, "and right now. Look. We'll have a cop in the hall downstairs all night; and the chances are that we'll be around for a couple of hours ourselves. So don't worry about him. He isn't coming back here. I promise you that — and I never meant anything so much in my life. Because when he did that to Paddy, when he — "

The haggard expression came back on him; as soon as he permitted himself to mention or even think of Ahern, it was all as bad as ever inside him.

"Oh, I'll be all right," Miss Stewart said, but not too evenly. "Just fine. But I don't think you should keep thinking and thinking about — about what happened tonight. It only — "

"Then tell me something," McCallister almost implored, putting to her in a low, hurried and tense voice

131

the questions which, so far, he had been unable to put to himself. "Do you think that's the end of him? Do you think he just died for nothing back there, like a dog in a gutter?"

"Oh, no!" She was shocked and very earnest at that. "I'm sure he didn't. Because — because there's the Lord, I feel. I don't know what I'd do if I thought there wasn't."

It was without doubt a very genuine assurance, and one that McCallister had wanted badly to find for himself, and for Ahern also. She stood looking up in that serious way, now obviously much concerned for him, not for herself, with the lamplight shining on her brown hair; and McCallister, using two fingers, brushed some of it back gently over her ear before suspecting that he wanted to do it at all. Taking his hand down again, he could only give her a twisted and miserable grin by way of excuse. "Crazy!" he said. "Didn't I tell you?"

But perhaps she understood him a little better at that moment than he understood himself.

"Oh, that's all right," she said softly. "Don't bother about it."

She went with him to the outside door; she even put her head through after him. "And you be careful," she said, anxious about that. There was warmth in McCallister then, his first warmth for quite a while; what he felt suddenly was that, in a few minutes, he had achieved a closer and much more comprehensible intimacy with her than on those other occasions in 8E when he had watched for the kitchen light and her white bathrobe —

just before daybreak then, and without this girl knowing a thing about it. No bigger than a dime, he thought; a kid, really; and yet having that rare human quality for quick and unforced compassion, showing it with Paddy Ahern a little while ago, and with him now.

But that was 8A, and what happened there to McCallister, and perhaps to her; in 8B, however, on the other side of the living room wall, conditions were much different. In that room, on the white modernistic divan where McCallister had watched her so often munching her candy and looking through her picture magazines, Mrs. Wheeler now sobbed helplessly, rocking back and forth with her doll-like brunette features all tear-sodden and woebegone, and with both arms hugging herself under the breasts. "Harry!" she was crooning as McCallister entered. "Oh, Harry! Why did they do this to you, Harry? Why did they murder you?"

Eckstrom compressed his already firm mouth. He occupied a ladder-back chair, placed several feet before her, in his usual seated position, very erect on it, hands clasping the insides of his thighs, elbows pointed out at a slight angle, head well up and both feet planted solidly on the rug under him.

"Now, madam," Eckstrom requested gruffly, "I'll thank you to pay attention to me like a sensible woman. I'm sorry for the trouble that's come to you — we all are; but if you're ready to help us now, as I hope you are, I'd say we'd better get on with it."

He was ignored.

133

"Harry!" Mrs. Wheeler moaned, crooning that name in a dreary and broken manner. "What are they talking about? I think they're trying to drive me out of my mind. Oh, Harry! Oh, God! Ohhh!"

Eckstrom, trying again, first lifted both hands and then dropped them in a gesture that bespoke exasperated futility.

"Did you love your husband?" he demanded almost ferociously. "And do you want us to catch the man who murdered him? That's the choice you have, madam; that's all there is. Now. He had a car downstairs tonight; we know that; and we can figure out for ourselves that it was a new car, one he bought in the last couple of days, if you're not able to tell us anything about it. All right; we've got that far. Let's go on. Somebody must know what kind of a car he bought — the color, the make, the model, even the registration. That's why I've asked you to tell me where he's been keeping himself, who the people were he stopped with, wherever he was. They'd know about the car. They could tell us in two minutes — "

She gulped for breath.

"If I knew!" she whispered at Eckstrom. "If I knew!"

He regarded her with the yellow and froglike eyes for about fifteen seconds — then rose, came over to McCallister, and drew him out to the apartment corridor.

"All I've heard," he said then, the tough voice rasping like chalk on a blackboard. "All there's been. Harry, Harry, Harry! Now it's possible, McCallister, that's she's not lying outright to me about the car, she just doesn't know anything about it; but she knows where the husband's been, and she's afraid to admit it. We'll have to chance something. Do you still have a key to our apartment with you?"

McCallister nodded.

"Then get over there," Eckstrom ordered. "She'll phone somebody the minute we leave; she'll want company or advice after this. And it's my contention that she'll call the place where Harry Wheeler was hiding out, to learn whether or not we're telling the truth about him coming around here tonight. She's been well drilled, do you see; she wouldn't believe any of us under oath. We could stay here all night working on her; but until she's sure in herself that the husband's dead, and that we're not just trying to pick up a lead to him, we won't be able to get anything useful out of her. All right, then. Get back to the apartment, and on those earphones; and I'll be over just as soon as I've put the fear of God into this one."

But of course, back in apartment 8E, there were many things waiting for McCallister. The chair Ahern had used night after night; a can of his pipe tobacco forgotten on the window sill; a pair of oversized black rubbers that he was never going to use any more. Pretty queer, McCallister thought numbly; just a couple of hours ago he had left this living room to talk to Paddy downstairs. And now . . .

He sat down in Sheridan's place, adjusting the earphones, and heard Eckstrom's growling voice rasp over to him from apartment 8B. The minutes began to tick by for him very slowly and quietly; but the one thing he never suspected, couldn't suspect, was that in the same manner, or perhaps even at greater length, they were ticking by now for Walter Sheridan in that back cellar of his on Narcissus Road.

It was pitch dark in there, icy cold; and every few minutes Sheridan felt compelled to check the hour against his wrist watch. He had a superstitious conviction now that on the dot of four, but only at that precise instant, there would be no danger for him in starting out after the convertible; and so little by little that four o'clock deadline began to build itself into safety assured for him. Ever since early that evening, when Harry Wheeler had been shot down against the convertible, Sheridan had undergone a series of crises each more intense and nerve-wracking than the preceding one; and the cumulative effect they produced at last on him was to make his mind work in erratic darts, seeing omens and portents everywhere, or else in brilliant flashes as sudden and uncontrolled by him as summer lightning.

He would find himself thinking one minute of that expensive-looking leather suitcase, then of Ahern, then of that girl who of course had spoiled everything for him. In the darkness and chill around him there was opportunity to remember her time after time with cold hate, to understand that every step he took from now on must be of necessity a perilous and uncertain one, and to reflect upon how heartbreakingly different it all could have been only for Miss Stewart. That phrase recurred every few seconds to him, even when he attempted impatiently to direct his thoughts from it. Only for her, only for her, only for her . . . She was how he explained his present position to himself — Ahern dead, almost certainly, he blamed for it, the convertible missing and the dangerous compulsion for Walter Sheridan of starting out now to look for it. He dropped a cigarette on the floor, thinking of her, and ground his shoe over it in a vicious half circle until there was nothing left of the butt except shreds and ashes. She was the one who had put herself in his way from the very beginning, not he in hers. There was a humming in his mind whenever he thought of that; and she came back to him time and again as the one focal point in all his misfortunes.

She had another effect on him: she made that last half hour which he had to spend in the cellar by far the longest. He moved up and down between the laundry machines, stamping his feet to warm them, and smoking with nervous and excited inhalations one cigarette after another. At four, not a moment ahead of time, nor a moment after, he raced up into the yard, not doing it slowly and cautiously, either, because if he had attempted it in that way he was afraid that he could not have done it at all. Yet nobody challenged him at the top of the steps, where he stopped short, expecting anything, to look around hurriedly; above him there was a great blaze of stars, and around him only unfinished apartment buildings with no light visible in any direction, and with

137

most of the upper rooms as yet scarcely more than squares and angles from the perspective of Sheridan's vantage point.

He was not in the street here, but in one of the rear areas around which had been designed every block in the development. Earlier, on his way to telephone Miss Stewart, he had utilized an inner square like this to avoid McCallister and Ahern behind 1775 Hawthorne Crescent; and he saw at once that the safe and sensible thing to do would be to use that means of approach now also.

Get into the building next door to 1775, he counseled himself, go up a flight or two and look down from the hall window to make sure that the convertible was waiting for him in the only place where Ahern should have left it. He determined on that procedure while edging out carefully from the building; and then in the open area wind roared up at him from one of the alleyways, bringing with it a dry stinging smell either of wood or cement dust. It was a savage wind now, raging through slotlike openings from the street, and then raging out again through the yard in enormous sailing blasts, sharp as a knife.

Sheridan clutched the Homburg against it, darting on in a half crouch with his other hand pressed in to his side, near the revolver. He was soon breathless. He stopped then by a building excavation, his gray eyes jumping down, suddenly startled and just as suddenly relieved, at a red lamp hanging from a trestle, and at a steam shovel beyond it that squatted crookedly asprawl with an air of idle but brooding menace, like the contraption of another planet; then he went on again. He came out on the first cross street up from Hawthorne Crescent, worked north a block, to approach 1775 from the other side; and here he had to risk showing himself for a moment on an inhabited street where arc lamps swung in the wind and tossed vast shadows up and across a parking ramp.

This intersection, which there was no way for him to avoid if he wanted to approach the buildings along Hawthorne Crescent from the rear, and not from the front, presented his first and only danger point. He stopped and watched for a few seconds, jumpily worried that he had to reveal himself now in order to get from one side of this avenue to the other. The wind hammered past him, and the tenanted apartment buildings across the road seemed to run on and on, the two entry lights at each door repeated endlessly, as if into a mirror. He was afraid to go out there under the lights; yet something took command of him, not his will, even against his will. He thought of Eckstrom and McCallister and all the rest of them, around here somewhere, perhaps waiting and watching; but what he had felt for them always, an invincible conviction of his own personal superiority, swept over him just when he needed it most. It was, and he remained acute enough to realize this, perhaps the last strong upward surge of his psychological pendulum; and he took advantage of it by grabbing his hat again, and then by dashing across the intersection to another apartment entrance on the far side.

He looked back there; he listened; he saw and heard nothing alarming. There was a room here in back of the elevator all littered, just as in 1775, with go-carts and baby carriages. He found steps there, steps leading down; he used them and slipped forward through another basement laundry. A door; more steps, up this time; and then another area like the one he had just left, with a dark central part, one or two lamps around, and a few other lights placed high up against the surrounding buildings.

He kept well out in the center, picking his way for himself, and pausing in the darkest places to watch back of him, and on all sides of him, before moving on again. No more than a sharp back angle of 1775 Hawthorne Crescent was presented to him in here; but he remained unworried about this now, because he remembered at once that from the Wheeler apartment, as from 8E, no rear view of the building could be obtained.

Then steps again in 1773 (the damn buildings like peas in a pod, Sheridan thought agitatedly); another basement laundry; and another room for the baby carriages. And then up two flights, the stairs warm here, brightly lit, shiningly hushed; out into a hall green and gold like 1775, with the same kind of brass knobs and apartment numerals glittering under an identical ceiling fixture, and the same kind of sand urn at each end of the same elevator door. And of course the hall window in the same place, and the maple bench in front of it, and the checked green curtains in back of it — all these items twinned to the corridor at 1775 in the most exact item by item duplicate.

He lifted the curtains half an inch aside at that window, pressing himself forward against the wall and keeping his head sidewise to it. The first automobile he recognized on the crescent, pointed towards this end of the street and almost directly below him, was Frank Eckstrom's. The second was the dark-green convertible.

PART FIVE

Sʜᴇʀɪᴅᴀɴ, now displaying deep lines of strain and fatigue around the mouth, took hold of the curtain with both hands, hung on it, and rolled the side of his face into it. All along he had insisted to himself that he knew where Ahern had parked the convertible, the one possible place; and yet he must never have been fully convinced that it would be left open and undefended to him in this manner. For a moment now his face rested against the curtain, eyes closed, lips working a bit; but then suddenly, remembering Eckstrom's coupé, he lifted the curtain again, came up on tiptoes and looked down along Hawthorne Crescent as far as permitted by his almost parallel angle of vision with it.

Why was that coupé still here? he asked himself anxiously. What were they doing? The gray eyes inspected both sides of the crescent with a hurried and stealthy flicker, as if they had begun to feel troubled by the suspicion of something half seen, or rather half suspected, in regard to the street under him. What? He discovered that he did not want to think about it, whatever it was.

Some hours ago he had failed with the girl because of a few seconds hesitancy and overcaution; this time, and for exactly the same motives, he understood that he must not chance failing with the convertible.

Action was needed here; the thing done, not deliberated over. So he ran back to the hall stairs, rounded the first turn in them — and stopped rigid the next instant with his feet on two different levels and his head twisted up and around to the second floor, over his shoulder. Wait a minute! Sheridan warned himself uneasily. He had seen no one on guard at the convertible, or near it; but wasn't that precisely what he would have seen if Eckstrom had been told about it by Mrs. Wheeler, and if Eckstrom were now watching it?

The impact of that possibility struck at him like a blow over the heart. Could they have got a description of that automobile from Mrs. Wheeler? Of course! And, if they had, wouldn't one of them have recognized it on the street down there, forced open the trunk and identified it beyond question as Harry Wheeler's? Only a minute ago Sheridan had felt positive that the convertible was the last step for him, if perhaps the most dangerous one; now, however, and reasoning from a similar basis, he saw just how simply and easily it might be the last step for Frank Eckstrom also.

He raced back again to the second floor, and from the window there looked down at the cars along the curb, the walk before 1775 — although the courtyard entrance itself was hidden from him — the narrow belts of shadow

143

under each window sill on the building opposite, and the high, curved arm of the street light at the corner of Parkway Oval. All this area quiet and apparently deserted at a few minutes past four in the morning; and of course, as Sheridan now began to see it, all just the way it would be if Frank Eckstrom was down there waiting for him.

He dropped the curtain, clasped his hands together savagely, put both of them to the side of his face — and then lifted the curtain again. Everything looked the same. It was all right, he tried to convince himself; the foolish thing would be to start worrying about Eckstrom now. Because if he did, if he imputed to that man knowledge and cunning that very probably had no existence in fact . . . But he could not help himself; the idea had come to him, and now the idea would not go away from him. Suppose they were disposed all around the convertible, ready and watching for the moment he showed himself? Perhaps a few hours ago they had accepted on strong factual evidence, or what looked like it, the belief that he had got away in the car; but what did they believe now? There was the point of this thing. What had Mrs. Wheeler been able to tell them of the convertible?

There was no way for Sheridan even to guess at that part; as soon as the problem had presented itself it became maddening to him. It might be that there was no one watching the car, no one suspicious of it; and it might be that it had been left there for only one purpose — to deliver him into their hands.

Something very unfortunate happened to him at this point: there occurred an abrupt and sickening reversal in his previous opinion of Frank Eckstrom. Now their intimate association for so many years became no longer a comfort to Sheridan, but frightening rather, because he knew so well, and could recall so well, the hacked, tough face, the rasping voice, the stupid-looking and yellowish eyes; and above all else the patience, the thoroughness, the experience, the quick mind and the lucid and often unerring decisions. He began to hate Eckstrom so much that his entire body trembled from it; then something much worse even than this happened to him. It was if he could hear Eckstrom's voice in the hall, growling at him over a faint whisper of steam in the radiators, and explaining the thing for McCallister and the others as he had so often explained matters like this to Sheridan himself.

"What can we do now?" Eckstrom was demanding, one forefinger uplifted in his usual cherubic gesture to command perfect attention. "What do you think? We decided first, like the pack of fools we all are, that he drove away in the car; but now we know that he never got his hands on it. Why? I can't tell you — not unless Ahern drove it around here before he was killed. Now Ahern didn't have the keys on him up there on Narcissus Road, so Mr. Sheridan took them, and I think I can tell you the reason for it. He's still after that car; he must still think that he's got some kind of a chance to get hold of the money. And I'll add this. I wouldn't be a damn bit surprised if he's looking for it all through the development right now; and leaving this street till the last just because he's afraid of it. All right. We can play it that way for Mr. Sheridan; we can leave that automobile where it is, and keep ourselves out of sight around it for the next couple of hours. It's a chance; I admit that. But if he does what I'm thinking — "

And at once those words heard only in Sheridan's mind became louder and more physically real to him than any dim echo of sound in the apartment corridor — became not words he imagined, but words he was now convinced must have passed in actual conversation. He was ready to accept a calculated risk, even anxious, provided that there was half a chance at success; but what was this? If they had located the car through Mrs. Wheeler's description of it, they had of course opened the trunk immediately and found Wheeler inside, and the money with him; and if they had the money in their possession, showing himself or not showing himself downstairs would be equally futile — at least for him. Not for them, though, since he would be doing the very thing which Frank Eckstrom might have counted upon. Then how could he handle it from this end? In what way, before making the attempt, could he be sure first that no one was watching the convertible?

Again he peered down haggardly into the street from behind his curtain. Twenty minutes past four now, time running out for him, and nothing tangible to seize upon down there, nothing to influence his decision either one way or the other. Chance it, Sheridan urged himself. Soon people would be getting up in these buildings, and workmen would be swarming around in the unfinished portion of the development that for a few hours last night had afforded him shelter. Where would he conceal himself then? What possible chance would remain for him? No, he decided, standing motionless with the Homburg dapper as ever, but with the good-looking thin face under it glistening waxlike from this intense effort at exact and logical thought. Now or never!

Then, as he still hesitated uncertainly, another idea came to him. Had he been out of his head? Why hadn't he understood at once that Eckstrom would never have left his coupé in plain sight if they were waiting to trap him? Relief blasted up in him. Again he broke for the stairs, obeying a fierce inward drive to get the thing over with; but then for the second time, and after no more than a step or two, he began to picture Eckstrom as that one vital half movement ahead of him, even there.

"He knows us," he heard Eckstrom growl, "and that means he knows we'd be busy around here for most of the night. Well, let's leave my car right where it is. Why? Because he'll figure then that we don't know anything about the convertible behind it, or else we'd get the coupé out of there and not scare him off from the attempt, anyway. We're dealing with Mr. Foxy Sheridan, remember; so the first thing we do that doesn't look right to him, the first slip we make that he can manage to put his finger on — "

147

Then the coupé was no good to Sheridan, either, since it could be argued with equal plausibility from both sides of the picture. Two choices, Sheridan saw dizzily — to go down there or not to go down there; and no third.

No third?

He fumbled at a fresh pack of cigarettes, almost dropping it as his mind jumped at that last angle. No third way at all? But why not? The watchers could be watched, maybe, and not left invisible where they were; because even at four in the morning, if you used your head, there was one way to . . .

It had come suddenly to him, as an inspiration. Into their hands, he repeated for his own benefit, but now with a feeling of triumphant and overwhelming assurance. Was that what they thought — counted upon? He started again for the basement laundry and the yard stairs, not turning back this time, and seeing at last how he could outmaneuver Frank Eckstrom even with everything set against him. It had become dazzlingly simple. The third way to do this, and the one perfectly safe way, had just opened itself up before Walter Sheridan like a glimpse at salvation.

In the living room of 8E, at this moment, McCallister sat back of the earphones, Eckstrom on the cot behind him, and Gus Bruder over at the picture window with the night glasses. They had listened by now, McCallister on the wire and the others at second hand, to a couple of outgoing phone calls from apartment 8B; but both of these had gone only to Mrs. Wheeler's mother over in Brooklyn. Even Eckstrom had been forced to accept them for what they obviously were: the resort of a bewildered and grief-stricken woman, alone over there at this time of morning, to the one person closest to her.

"But I'll tell you what's in her mind," Eckstrom insisted doggedly after the second one. "She's asking herself if we only thought up a story like this to get some kind of a lead onto the husband. She's afraid to call him, afraid we can trace it some way; but she's not iron, McCallister. I'll give her just about — How is she acting?" he barked suddenly at Gus Bruder. "What is she doing over there?"

"Walkin' up and down," his driver told him. "Up and down. Wipin' her eyes. And — Oh-oh. Over at the phone now. Take it, Richie."

Their pickup tinkled.

"Here it comes," McCallister said. "She's calling Long Distance."

He tightened up inside with a cold gripe. Was this at last —

"Then it's what we're waiting for," Eckstrom said. He got up quickly. "First get it all, McCallister; then tell it all. I don't want you to miss a word."

The Long Distance operator came on.

"Atlantic City," McCallister said, a little breathless now. "She wants a hotel down there. The — "

Eckstrom, moving around the table, pointed to the earphones and then put a finger to his lips to suggest

149

complete attention to the matter at hand; and McCallister nodded, veiling his dark blue eyes at the same time as if to strengthen one sense by denying another.

He listened intently, both hands holding the earphones against his head; while Eckstrom, in what must have been a considerable effort for him, watched McCallister's facial expression without a word or even an inquiring forward thrust of the chin. Then McCallister pushed his chair back and yanked his neck from under the earphones.

"The Hotel Alcott," he said. "She got the night clerk."

Eckstrom bent forward.

"Who did she want to talk to? The husband?"

"Somebody named Bennett," McCallister said. "Only he checked out early this afternoon."

"Now she's just sitting there," Bruder announced. "White as a ghost, Lieutenant. All — "

"The husband," Eckstrom asserted grimly. "Of course. Now she knows."

"Beginnin' to bawl," Bruder volunteered. "Sittin' there and — "

"Leave her alone," Eckstrom growled at him. "Or are you enjoying it? Stop watching the woman now. Don't you have the decency to — Hello!" He had grabbed up the foyer telephone. "Long Distance? I want the Hotel Alcott in Atlantic City, New Jersey. That's right. The Hotel Alcott."

"I thought you wanted to know," Bruder said, sullen about it. "You did before."

"Because I had to," Eckstrom rasped cuttingly. "Not because I wanted to. There's the difference. And if you're thickheaded enough not to see it — Hello! Yes, I'm on here. What?"

There was a short wait during which McCallister rolled a cigarette around between dry lips; then the Alcott came on, and Eckstrom and the night clerk down there began what appeared to be a very unsatisfactory conversation.

"His name," Eckstrom said, "and his room number, and his New York address — No, I don't want them. I want information about his car. His car!" He listened, staring ahead of him at the blank wall of the foyer. "Then put me through to your night man at the garage," he said. "Yes, right now. When did you think?"

He was given the garage; and he was informed there, the words echoing thinly back to McCallister, that no car had been registered last night, or for the previous week, under the name of Bennett. "Then get me the hotel manager," Eckstrom said. "Yes, I know what time it is. Wake him up!" He had to wait again. His cheeks shone a bit and that asthmatic breathing of his vibrated the mouthpiece.

"Anything you can tell me about that automobile," he said, after the manager had come on. "Yes, it's important. Why do you suppose you have the New York Police Department on your telephone at this hour of night? No, your garage couldn't tell me anything about it — I tried there. But I thought you might be able to get me some-

151

one who — " He listened again. The bulldog jaw hardened.

"Then can you get me the doorman?" he said. "Yes. When the hell did you think?" He looked up at McCallister. "At this hour!" he said. "At this hour!" He was sweating. He added a very coarse expletive, a rare thing with Frank Eckstrom, and one which indicated how much dependence he had placed on this conversation.

"Hello!" he said. "No phone. And you can't — What? I just wanted to know if he'd ever been seen driving an automobile down there. And if — No, your clerk couldn't tell me. I think he has your kind of head. That's right. Your kind of head."

The mechanical, whining edge of that other voice sputtered at him, outraged.

"One of the biggest hotels in Atlantic City," Eckstrom said, savage now with the only lead he had got so far slipping away through his fingers. "I see. No, I didn't expect you to know all of your guests personally; but I thought you'd have some kind of information about the people you seem to harbor down there. Yes — harbor. A man in and out of your hotel for two weeks and you can't find anybody to tell me if — Thanks," he said, the mouthpiece vibrating audibly and painfully now even to McCallister. "You're a credit to your profession. Yes," he said, his voice rising. "That's what I told you. That's what I think of you."

He hung up.

"They might get it down at Norton's," Gus Bruder

said. "You sent Stein and Jack Hennessey down there, didn't you? I wouldn't — "

Eckstrom looked at him. He stopped quickly.

"All right," he said. "All right! I was just — "

McCallister said nothing, understanding that after all this nerve-wracking wait they were now just where they had been two hours ago — further back, even, since Sheridan had been given the opportunity to lengthen out his start on them minute by minute. "Now what do you want to do?" Eckstrom snarled at him, catching the expression of that thought immediately on McCallister's face. "Give it up? Well, I'll tell you something about Mr. Sheridan, and about this. I've not even started."

He went back to the telephone, calling downtown in for consultation and advice. "I know that," he said, not overly respectful there, either. "Yes. I'll call the police down there as soon as I've finished with you. But I don't think — What? All right. What do I know? I'm only — " He listened; he hung up, or banged up, his ruddy face all congested; then he kicked his chair back.

"I hope to God," he said, quietly but harshly, and without looking this time at McCallister, "that one of you realizes if he had been a police officer instead of a fool, we wouldn't be beating our brains around trying to find out what kind of a car it was. We'd know."

McCallister could not answer him. He knew that Eckstrom had sent that remark in his direction; he knew he deserved it. He went into the bedroom and looked down from the front window at Eckstrom's coupé and the

153

canvas top of a new green convertible. Where to try? he asked himself dully. Where even to start?

Included as part of the over-all plan for Parkway Heights was a total of four garages, one located in each quarter of the development to serve quickly and efficiently that particular area; but as yet only one of these had been opened for business. It lay at the back of a cross street three blocks north and two west of 1775 Hawthorne Crescent. A broad entrance ramp, well illuminated and therefore prominent from blocks away, led up to it from the corner; but just beyond this, protected by the shadow of the higher driveway and lit only by a dim bulb at the point of admission, a service underpass led down and around to the basement level. This underpass was the one Sheridan used. He dropped into it from the side, over a shallow protecting wall, landed on hands and knees and crouched rigidly in that position, straining to catch the first hint of pursuit or detection from any point in the surrounding neighborhood. None came to him. He eased erect, his breath quieting down slowly. Half done now, he comforted himself, and yet no one had seen him on the way over; why then, provided that he was equally careful, should anyone notice him on the way back?

He slipped down to the basement archway, and from there made a hurried reconnaissance of the garage interior. An attendant upstairs, he concluded — but none here. He moved inside then, straightened the white scarf,

154

tilted the Homburg nervously, and edged past car fenders and a line of bulky concrete pillars to the stairway over in one corner.

He ascended these with intent care, listening and watching all the time for activity overhead. On the upper level he again paused. There was a small office across from him, empty but brightly lit; a couple of gas pumps beyond this; and way over in one of the corners, near the elevator, an attendant in work clothes and glistening rubber boots. This man, who had his back to the stairway, was whistling to himself and hosing off a gunmetal sedan; and he did not see or hear anything unusual until Sheridan came up behind him as if from the main entrance.

They conversed, the attendant wiping his hands on a bit of waste. "So I thought you could pick it up for me," Sheridan told him, the importance of what he had to do now, and without arousing suspicion, pressing at him so that his left hand clenched into a fist in his overcoat pocket. This was it, this was all there was, this was safety and perhaps final deliverance for Walter Sheridan — or else the whole thing to start over again, if that was even remotely possible, from a different angle. He grinned painfully at the attendant, with great effort. "Should have driven it up myself," he said. "I know. But I thought maybe you wouldn't have room for me. And I'm pooped, Jack; I just got in from Washington with the missus."

"I don't know," the attendant informed him, stolidly obstinate in the knowledge of his exact duties and responsibilities. "I'm all alone here till seven o'clock, mister. And I ain't supposed to —"

Seven o'clock! Sheridan thought. He took a very deep breath.

"For a buck?" he said. "I'm not just throwing it at you. I'll listen to reason."

"Well, for a buck," the attendant said. "That's a little bit different. The guys that come in here, and the things they want you to do for nothing —" He swung a pad around on a stand-up desk, laid his cigarette on the edge and wrote down the name and address that Sheridan gave him at 1775 Hawthorne Crescent.

"Right in front of the building," Sheridan told him, his head aching, the grin fixed clumsily on his lips. "You can't miss it. It's a dark-green Buick convertible — the big job. And thanks for helping me out on it, Jack. Thanks a million."

He detached Harry Wheeler's ignition key from the leather folder.

"And I'd like you to pick it up soon as you can," he said. "It worries me leaving it out like this. I got things in it."

"Ten minutes," the attendant said. "Maybe fifteen. I got to lock up around here and finish the wash job."

"Okay," Sheridan nodded at him, not pushing the thing too much. "Swell. Just as long as you get it."

Then there was a bad minute or so when the garageman opened the outer door for him, and he had to walk down that brightly lit entrance ramp like any late cus-

156

tomer. His gray eyes jumped around in all directions, he crossed the road quickly, and on the next side street made at once for the nearest apartment vestibule. From there on he kept to the back areas, as he had on the way over, so that only at intersections was it necessary to show himself for a few moments out in the open. He crossed two of these without event, after watching his chance; but at the third a milkman carrying an empty tray came out of a building just as Sheridan was about to enter it. He stopped short. His fingers touched the gun in his overcoat pocket, and tightened around it.

"Cold mornin'," the milkman said, nodding at him. Then he went by, and Sheridan looked at his back. Easy, he cautioned himself; Eckstrom was over on Hawthorne Crescent, and not around here. So — Still he hesitated, uncertain about this; but in the end it seemed to him that the best way to handle it was to let it pass. What could he do with the milkman? Take him along? Or leave him dumped in some hallway to be found there, and perhaps to attract Eckstrom's attention? He went on again, even more careful now; but at ten minutes of five he was back safe in that second-floor hallway of his overlooking Hawthorne Crescent.

The milkman bothered him a bit, but not too much. What else could he have done back there? Sheridan reflected anxiously. It was obvious that the milkman knew nothing about him, because then he would have betrayed something. Letting him go, Sheridan decided, had been the smart thing. His route was back there on

Arlington Drive, blocks away; and he could know no more about Eckstrom at this moment, and Eckstrom's problem, than Eckstrom knew about him.

Just a break now, Sheridan thought wearily — just one break! From his window he saw that the convertible and Eckstrom's coupé were still in position, and this strengthened his belief that in a few minutes now there was only one of two things that could possibly happen. Either the garage attendant would be stopped and questioned as soon as he unlocked the convertible door, which would mean that Eckstrom had been watching it all this time; or else no one would pay the least attention to him. So it was not Sheridan in the end who would have to turn up the last card for Frank Eckstrom; but Eckstrom who would have to do it for him.

Then if they stopped the attendant, to get the story from him, they could rush over to the garage in their cars, surround it, and search the place inch by inch — only, of course, Walter Sheridan had not been quite so stupid as to hang over there waiting for them. The great Eckstrom! he thought contemptuously again. He sat down on the maple bench, drawing at a cigarette in quick, nervous inhalations; he touched his tongue to his lips and twisted himself from one side to the other, his hands clamping down on the hard wood; then he had to get up again. Jumpy as McCallister, he thought.

He could not help it. He pictured the garageman driving away from here in the convertible, unquestioned and unchallenged, and then himself slipping across these yards for the last time. Another buck to the guy; some story as to why he needed the car right away; and then everything done. He reseated himself on the bench, and then jumped up immediately to re-examine the crescent. Five or ten minutes now; a bit longer, perhaps; but then surely . . .

He kept moving from the bench to the window, back to the bench, back anxiously to the window. In him, pounding away like a drum, but still heard in that deserted apartment corridor only by Sheridan himself, he began to feel short, rapid thumps as his heart tried to adjust itself to his increasing nervous and muscular tension. He closed his eyes for a few seconds, rubbing his forehead between them with one knuckle, and suddenly realized how dead-tired he was. One minute went by; two; three; and then while he waited beside that hall window with his eyes constantly watching the courtyard walk at 1775, there was a rather peculiar extension of him in another place, and without his knowledge.

It seemed that he appeared suddenly, wraithlike in outline and still appallingly real, in an eighth-floor bedroom just next door to him on the crescent. There was an opening in that room where there had been solid wall a moment ago; and from this Sheridan now appeared to be looking out and down without a flicker of the stony gray eyes at little Jane Stewart.

She knew who he was. She tried at once to move or to speak, to call out to someone; but she could not. Behind him the wall continued to blur apart, making visible at his back a narrow passage along which he must have been projected just now without the least sound. It seemed to her that she knew everything about the passage; and knew best of all, but a little too late, that she should have remembered to tell McCallister about it, because it had always been hidden there on one side of the bedroom, and always waiting for Walter Sheridan.

He detached the white scarf from around his throat, still watching her silently and without expression. He came forward with it, smoothing it, and she ran from him into a space that extended miraculously through the apartment, on and on; yet also, with the other half of a double consciousness, and in a complete paralysis of mind and action, watching all this from her own bed in her own bedroom. The shadow of his upper body and of the Homburg, giant-sized, loomed up fantastically over her. She sobbed, trying to fight him, and heard the vile and incomprehensible sentence he breathed at her; but this in her head, somehow, and not audibly. She heard McCallister shouting her name, far distant; she answered him; then she tore free from the one behind her with a supreme effort.

She began crying out in her throat, whimpering, while in another sequence, and in what seemed to be the most natural transposition of scene and action, he glided at her from the Wheeler apartment with the darkness of the passage advancing along with him, and at last hovering above him so that nothing could be seen in it but the merciless cold features, the white scarf and the two hands reaching down for her.

She screamed then. She sat up dazedly, tasting the scream clogged and thick in her throat, and saw the bedroom all safely familiar around her, no secret passage in it, no Sheridan; only the curtains fluttering at the courtyard window, and Molly Burnett's bed neat and empty beside her. She looked around, not quite awake yet, and whimpering to herself in slower and slower gasps. Then she lay down again, pulling the blankets all the way up to her chin, and watching that closet corner, where the secret passage had been a moment ago, with fixed and wide-open brown eyes.

She discovered that the bed was warm and cozy around her, but she icy cold somehow. Her teeth clicked together; she listened for some kind of human and comforting sound, any kind; but for companionship at this hour she heard only the wind in the courtyard, and a persistent low thrum from the kitchen refrigerator. It became clear to her that if she closed her eyes now, if she attempted to sleep again, Sheridan would be waiting for her; and so she got up out of bed, shivering, and padded out that way to the kitchen in bathrobe and slippers.

Even with the light on there she spilled half of the hot milk she was trying to pour for herself; the kitchen glare seemed cold and hard to her then, nakedly brutal against the white walls; and she learned at once that the worst part of the night was now beginning for her in the obscure torture chamber of mind and nerves.

She went back to the living room, leaving the kitchen light on behind her, and sat there in the dark with her cup of milk forgotten on the end table. She felt more alone than she ever had, and more frightened also. They had left her to this now, even McCallister; it was all quite plain because from the other side of the courtyard, from 8E, nothing but a row of blank windows stared back at her against this five-in-the-morning blackness. And downstairs, where they had promised to leave a policeman, the courtyard walk curved emptily around to the crescent, and the crescent out to the tree shadows near Parkway Oval.

The deathly cold wouldn't go out of her; her lips quivered. There was a man who hated her, and who wanted to kill her; and yet not one of them, not even Richie McCallister, could be bothered about it. Her throat became painfully swollen. What was he doing at this moment, when she needed him most of all? And where was the man who . . .

Someone tapped on the hall door. She froze, thinking dumbly of the foyer telephone and outside assistance; but then, as helplessly compelled to do this as in her dream, she knew that she would have to see who was out there. She got up, shaky in the legs; she went two or three steps, two or three more; she saw that the door was chained, started breathing again, and at last forced her head down toward the tiny peephole of one-way

162

glass. Then she began shaking again, her teeth chattered, her heart jumped and caught and almost stopped for an instant. It was not the Homburg and the gray eyes out there, waiting for her, and of course perfectly aware, door or no door, that she was crouched inside watching and listening. It was Richie McCallister.

He tapped again, his small sober features harassed and uneasy, his very dark blue eyes searching one end of the corridor outside and then the other. He bit his lips. He tapped the third time, anxiously; but she could do nothing at all until she had leaned into the door and rested her head against it. After this she opened to him — to that Richie McCallister who had almost, but not quite, betrayed and abandoned her. "Well," she said. She stepped back, touching the brown hair, keeping her eyes away from him, and gathering the bathrobe at her waist with an angry and shaky gesture. "So you're still around, are you? That's a surprise."

"Saw your lights," McCallister muttered. "Thought I'd see how you were. Can't you sleep?"

He had known that it was going to be a very difficult interview at this hour, and under these conditions; but now he became uncomfortably aware that she had no intention of making it easier for him. She kept her face turned away, dead set against him. She would say nothing. As if he had remembered her, she thought, her eyes blurring. As if he hadn't come over here only to find out something the Lieutenant wanted to know, and not by any means for the reason he said.

163

He dropped his hat on the foyer table.

"That's no thing," he said, more uneasy than ever. "Sitting here in the dark. Worrying about him. When I told you — "

"Yes," she said, her throat drying up on her. "You told me a lot of things. And then — "

She went out past him to the kitchen. He hesitated, giving a nervous and impatient turn to the small head, because there were so many things he wanted to do for this girl; and because he knew, under these circumstances, how very little he could permit himself to offer her. How many times had they talked together? Twice, McCallister remembered. And so — The cup of milk caught his attention. He picked it up and followed her out to the kitchen.

"You fixed it," he said. "I was watching you. Then why didn't you drink it?"

"Because I didn't want it," she said. She had to wink her eyes several times. "And I don't want it. And what do you care?"

McCallister understood then that he was being accused of something. But what?

"Maybe I just don't like you sitting up by yourself," he said uneasily. "It gets me all — "

"Oh, of course," she said, looking straight in front of her with that cold and withdrawn expression. "You're just worried to death. Then why didn't you come over before to see how I was? But I don't matter to anybody," she said, her voice wavering on that sentence, and on the succeeding ones. "Who am I? A zero, that's all. I can lie over here all night and — "

She was not alone any more; she had McCallister with her; but that fact, instead of helping, sparked off and then sent immediately out of control the self-pity which had almost overwhelmed her before in the living room. She began to weep suddenly and helplessly for herself, dumbfounding McCallister. At the same time, however, she didn't want him to see it, wouldn't let him after the way he had acted — never! But when she had plunged blindly from her chair into the bedroom passage he caught up with her after a step or two. "Leave me alone!" she said, struggling against him. "Because that's all you did, anyway — all you cared. Let me go!"

"What are you acting like this for?" he whispered huskily. "When you know I — "

"Yes, I know," she said, despising him now for what he had proved to be, and for the way he had lied to her. "I know a lot of things I never suspected till now. You used to watch me, didn't you, and you used to think about me; and then you couldn't even be bothered to — "

"I'd have come over before!" McCallister said, getting her by the two shoulders. "But how could I? I had things to do; and I was afraid you might think — I know I ought to be shot! I could tell you were keeping it all inside you! But what could I do about it? You hardly know me. So how could I bust in over here? Just tell me that! How could I?"

"Go on," she said, weeping quietly again. "Go on and

pretend to me. That's been the story you've had all along. Act as if — "

"Act?" he said, frantic to convince her now. "Act? When I — " All his imposed caution and professional resolution went away somewhere, and he began groping gently around the back of her head, in desperation for the right way to explain himself.

"I took two sleeping pills," she whispered, after forcing down a couple of oversized swallows. "I thought they'd help me. And then I dreamt about him, and I had to get up, and I couldn't see any light over in your place. That's how you lied to me, I thought. That's how you went and left me just when — "

"Left you!" McCallister breathed. He tightened his arms. "You don't know what you're talking about! Do you suppose I'd ever do that? Do you think — "

All this was passing from one to the other in hurried whispers, the bedroom door glimmering dull-white in back of them, the secret and mysterious intimacy of five in the morning around them. The apartment seemed to be soundless and listening, the house also; only through the courtyard outside wind scuttered in uneasy and furtive whispers.

"Nobody with me," she wailed, a bit calmer, however, with a feeling in her that perhaps she hadn't needed anyone very much but McCallister himself. "And everything so quiet in here, so ready if he decided to come back again. That's all I could think of. You somewhere, and that Sheridan — Oh, Richie!" she said. "Richie!"

She clung to him. But then she had been in a very dark and frightening place when McCallister found her, and the way back from it was proving difficult and involved. It did not matter that she was important to herself; what she needed to feel now was that she had become important to him — that if Sheridan hated her, there was someone who loved her. So she whispered to him, and clung to him; and then started accusing him again, in breathless sentences never quite finished, of pretending to her, of lying to her and of abandoning her in the most callous and cold-blooded manner.

"When I tried to think up ways to meet you," McCallister whispered back, addressing those words with a kind of despairing intensity at the bedroom door. "When I even talked to you in my head, sometimes! But I didn't know what you thought of me. Watch it! I kept telling myself. Push yourself on a girl like that and — "

"A girl like that!" little Miss Stewart said. "Oh, yes! I'm so extraordinary. Well, I'm going to get out of here," she said, honking piteously into a tissue she produced from one of the bathrobe pockets. "Then none of you will have to bother his head about me. And you can do what you did before, Richie McCallister — you can leave me alone."

She understood what she wanted from him: an overwhelming protest or affirmation to cherish in her against everything that had to do with Walter Sheridan. Cunning about it, despising herself but not able to stop herself, she shook her head at him time after time even

167

while listening to anxiously murmured expressions of tenderness and devotion given over and over — beyond conviction from him, apparently, and because of her own need beyond shame from herself.

"Watching people!" she said, as if that was one thing she could never bring herself to forgive him for. "Spying on them, because that's what it amounted to, actually; and then trying to make them think — Oh, you don't have to keep lying to me. I know it's the easy way out for you, and I know I'm begging for it. I'm wonderful, I suppose; all you had to do was to look once at me through those night glasses. Then — "

"Sssh," McCallister murmured. He kissed her gently somewhere up on top of the left cheekbone. "Stop it. Just be quiet a minute."

She searched those small, sharp features of his from ear to ear, and must have seen in them exactly what she wanted to see. Then she pushed away, doing things to her hair, and studying him again in quick and rather abashed side glances.

"Acting like this," she said. "And at this hour! I don't know what you're going to think about me. I'm not even dressed."

But McCallister had now become serious and authoritative with her.

"You're not going to stay around here any more," he ordered flatly. "I won't let you; so that's out. And you wouldn't sleep, anyway. You know you wouldn't."

"Not in broad daylight," she agreed, shivering. "I

168

guess I could go up to my sister's in White Plains, only Burnett took the car tonight. And I'm afraid the trains won't be running for — "

"Okay," McCallister told her, cutting her off sharply. "I can get you a car, if that's all you need. Ed Brady just got hold of a couple of men downtown for the boss, and drove them up here in his Chevvy. He'll lend it to me — but I can't drive you, though. Because the Lieutenant got an idea we ought to scout through this whole neighborhood to see what we find. It's a chance to pick up something. And I guess it's about the only chance we have left."

Her eyes darkened underneath, swiftly.

"You mean he might still be around here?"

"Not unless he's crazy," McCallister told her grimly. "No. It's not that. It's kind of the last hope for tonight, that's all. We've been stopped cold everyplace else; but with Brady and the other fellows we can spread out a little and cover this development right. Somebody might have spotted him and the car. A watchman, maybe; or — "

"Then I want you to be careful," she said, anxious again. "He might be hurt somewhere, just watching for you. Please, Richie. Promise me!"

"That's what I've been hoping," McCallister said, his voice dropping to an extremely soft, even pitch. "That he's still around here. And don't worry about me; I'll be all right. Just get dressed. I'll go down right now and see Brady about the car."

169

He left her. The self-service elevator took him downstairs, and at the end of the courtyard walk he found Eckstrom talking to Ed Brady and the other reinforcements.

"What we're looking for," Eckstrom admitted heavily, "I don't know. But we'll start up on Narcissus Road, and fan out from there. Now what I want you to do — "

He went into more detailed explanation, and McCallister drew Ed Brady aside.

"Sure," Brady said. "Let her take it. But you'll have to pick it up for me first thing tomorrow, Richie. You know it? It's that beaten-up little Chevvy over there. Here's the key."

A squad car raced up from the direction of Narcissus Road. It stopped in the street, motor idling, and two uniformed cops and a milkman piled out of it. Eckstrom rumbled at them. They answered him. "What?" Eckstrom said. That one word cracked out over Hawthorne Crescent like a pistol shot. McCallister turned quickly toward him; so did Brady.

"I'm telling you," the milkman insisted to all of them. "One of those Homburg hats and a blue overcoat. I saw the guy! And I knew there was something funny about him, because he acted like he was just waitin' for me to look at him cockeyed. 'Cold mornin', I says. And he keeps turnin' to watch after me like — "

"Where?" Eckstrom demanded, that square jaw of his thrusting itself forward like so much rock granite. "And when?"

170

"A blond guy," the milkman said. "One of those sharp faces. My size. Where? Up on Arlington Drive maybe twenty, twenty-five minutes ago. I think about him. Then a couple of streets down I bump into your cops here, and they ask me — "

But detailed explanations were not required for Eckstrom, or for anyone else. Gus Bruder was hurriedly instructed to call the precinct for additional uniformed help; the squad car raced away to block off Eckington Street; and Brady's men, using the police sedan that had been parked on the other side of Hawthorne Crescent day and night for three weeks, roared off to block any outbreak on foot through the lots lying north and east around the development.

"Because we have to keep him inside now!" Eckstrom insisted passionately, even his excitement not quite so controlled as usual. "Inside this project! That's the first thing. Bottle him up! What he's doing around here, I don't know, and can't guess; but by God he's not slipping away on us this time! Where's Arlington Drive?"

The milkman sputtered directions. McCallister, who had listened to all this dumbly, with a dirty paling under his skin and a delicate but repeated touch of tongue against lips, woke up and sprinted back to the patrolman on duty in the vestibule at 1775.

"That nurse is coming downstairs!" he said. "That little one who was with us before on Narcissus Road. Put her into Ed Brady's car — that two-door sedan over

171

there — and get her started; and then come up after us to Arlington Drive. I think we got him!"

Outside Eckstrom and Mahoney were already seated and waiting in the coupé; and McCallister, running for it, almost knocked over a garage man who had just fastened his motorcycle to the back of a big green convertible. Mahoney backed the coupé from this man, smashed his gears into forward, swung around the motorcycle and whined off for Arlington Drive; and up at a second-floor window in 1773, not a hundred feet from the courtyard walk where all this furious activity had erupted seconds ago, Walter Sheridan looked down at it with his body flattened against the corridor wall and his heart pounding away inside him like a triphammer.

He was invisible from the street; but he had been able to watch everything that went on in it by means of his one-inch opening between the wall and the curtain. He had recognized the milkman at once, sweating, had watched his vividly pantomimed excitement, the way he nodded at Eckstrom and the others, insisted and pointed back to Arlington Drive; and then in the midst of all this, with Eckstrom barking orders at everyone, the garage man had finally appeared on his motorcycle.

And that was when Sheridan had felt in him a sickening upsurge of acute physical nausea. Because not one of them, not even Frank Eckstrom, so much as glanced at the garage attendant. He watched them curiously, cap pushed up, cigarette in mouth; he even asked a question of one of the uniformed men; but he was ignored, hustled around and pushed out of the way impatiently. McCallister ran back to 1775 for some reason. Then he sprinted out again, careened into the garageman, shoved away; and the next moment, in Eckstrom's coupé, they were all roaring north in the direction of Arlington Drive.

The milkman started off after them on foot, wanting to be in on the end of this; the last uniformed cop, after hesitating uncertainly for a moment, obeyed McCallister and trotted back up the walk to 1775. So two minutes ago there had been eight or nine very excited men milling around on the pavement; and now there was one, but to Walter Sheridan a vitally important one.

Looking after the coupé, and unlocking the convertible door slowly, the garageman shook his head and flipped his cigarette away just as Sheridan, up in 1773, made a belated and desperate rush for the hall stairs. Stop him! Sheridan thought madly. Stop him! Stop him! Stop him! The search would start from Arlington Drive now, and spread out from there; and of course this meant that Eckstrom and McCallister, with some of the others, from now on would be directly between him and the Parkway Heights garage.

He became heedless of noise, of proper caution, of anything; all he understood was that he had to get to the car now, before the attendant took it away, and before Eckstrom had a chance to complete his arrangements. They knew he was in here; Eckstrom must have summoned more help immediately; and how on foot, with all of them scattering out through the development, could Sheridan hope to get within shouting distance of the Parkway Heights garage, and of the money?

It was blindingly clear now that he had to get to the car in this street, and away in it while their attention was still concentrated on Arlington Drive; so he descended the stairs in great leaps, maddened by his own grievous and perhaps fatal misjudgment about the convertible. They had never known a thing about it — never suspected! And what had he done with the money down there waiting for him? Watched, sneaked around, backed off; when all the time — He sobbed drunkenly, his face all twisting up; now the only refuge he had was headlong and insane recklessness. He burst out into the vestibule at 1773, his knees buckling under him from downward momentum; he dropped his gun; he staggered and clawed for it, got up, slipped, caught himself and plunged ahead for the street door.

But the first thing he saw outside were the convertible taillights winking away from him around Hawthorne Crescent. He lifted the gun; he almost fired at that car. Then he stopped. Everything went out of him. He grinned nervously, not knowing it. He trotted a few steps. He stopped again. Narcissus Road lay empty before him, no police car visible on it, and of course no convertible.

He ran back into Hawthorne Crescent. Use a phone, he thought; tell the guy he wanted that convertible right now, and get him to bring it around to some street where — A phone? What phone, at five o'clock in the morning? They were all around him, in every apartment; but how could he get to one without —

He squeezed his jaws together with both hands. Just think it out, he urged himself frantically. There must be some phone around here that — Two people came down the courtyard walk from 1775. One was the cop on duty. The other was little Miss Stewart.

But Sheridan had heard them before they had a chance to see him. He got in between two of the parked cars, crouching there, with one hand on the fender and the other holding his revolver up and ready. He heard their steps coming towards him. He moved quickly, quietly. The steps stopped. They stopped at the car down from him. " — somewhere up there," he heard the cop say. "That's right, lady. You all right now?"

"I don't know," Jane Stewart confessed shakily. "I'm all — What did Mr. McCallister want me to do? Stay here?"

"I think you'd better go," the cop said. "That's what he told me. To start you off."

"All right," she said. "Is this — "

"Yop," the cop told her. "That's Brady's. Okay, now. You want Richie to call you?"

"Yes," she said. "Oh, yes! The minute it's over."

Then the cop ran off toward Narcissus Road, going by one side of a light pickup truck while Sheridan ducked down and away from him on the other. A car door opened. Sheridan moved again, still crouching; but then

175

in half an instant he glimpsed the incredible fact that he had been practically handed a car and a driver now, and perhaps a way to get to the Parkway Heights garage before any of them.

A motor ground. He slipped past the front of the pickup truck, edged down from it, made sure that the cop had vanished, and in one rush made the street side of a brown two-door sedan. It was just starting to back away from him, to turn out, but Sheridan was much too quick to allow that. He grabbed at the door handle; and Jane Stewart, hunched up anxiously in a seat that was much too big for her, turned her head towards him, and saw who it was.

Again, as by the lots earlier, she was given the breath of a chance; and again she missed it. She did then the one thing she should never have done. She stalled the engine.

PART SIX

AND AFTER THAT it was like the dream all over again, the thing taking place here and now when it could not possibly be so, any of it. She snatched at the ignition key, thinking to throw it into the road from him; her fingers slipped from the metal; it fell; and immediately after this Sheridan yanked the door open, and squirmed in beside her with a kind of lunatic quickness and intensity.

"Where did they go?" he demanded hurriedly, kneeling low on the front seat so that he could watch the corner of Narcissus Road around which the last of them, the uniformed patrolman, had just vanished. "And who saw me? That milkman, wasn't it?"

But the uproar he had watched earlier from his hallway observation point at 1773 had already given him the only information he needed. He'd better get to the garage, Sheridan decided now, attempting frantically to consider everything in half a second; and get to it as soon as possible, while they were still looking for him on Arlington Drive. A car had been provided for him, which meant the acquisition inside the development of quickness and mobility equal to theirs; and by means of that car he might be able to circle around them even now, using the oval, and approaching the Parkway Heights garage from the south side, the unprotected side, before they had a chance to work up that far.

"Get this thing started again!" Sheridan said, his left arm bracing him forward against the dashboard. "Right now. And I'm telling you something! You're the one got me into this, me and Ahern; but now I swear to Christ that you're the one getting me out of it. Where's that key?"

She made an attempt to grab it from the seat between them; but before she could touch it Sheridan had snatched at her wrist, twisting it down and back cruelly.

"Try to get rid of it," he said, "and I'll put a bullet through you. Just try it!" His whole face glistened. "You're one thing I'm gonna fix before any of them gets his hands on Walter Sheridan; because this time I'm ready for you, and for them, too. Start this car!"

Somewhere in the dream, bad as it was, there had been McCallister — but not here; and so she fought to open the door on her side, kicking and thrusting at him until Sheridan at last flung her around on the seat with both her shoulders pinned back against it, and with her face terrified and transfixed under his.

"Are you going to start it?" he said. "Are you?"

He lifted the gun up, crouching over her on one knee with the gray eyes savagely pinpointed under his Homburg. "You little bitch!" he said, still maddened at the thought of how that convertible had been left here by the curb for hour after hour, with none of them even suspecting what car it was, and with Sheridan himself stupidly afraid to go anywhere near. "You sneaking little bitch! But I'm gonna get out of this now — or you won't. Do you hear what I'm telling you? Now start this car!"

Some kind of common-sense reaction came into her; she managed to nod at him. Then she fumbled at the ignition lock, stiff-fingered, telling herself that the others were all around here now, and all looking for him. The thing to do, therefore, was whatever he wanted, at least temporarily; and then, when they were seen . . . The motor ground, pulled and turned over.

"I want you to go down to the oval," Sheridan ordered breathlessly, "and start around it. All the way right, till I tell you to turn in. Or do you know where the garage is back there past Eckington street?"

She forced out another nod.

"That's where we're going," Sheridan told her, still anxiously watching Narcissus Road. "So back this around, and do what I tell you to do. And don't forget for one second that I'm gonna take care of you first, if anything happens. You bitch! You rotten little tramp!"

He began spewing out at her panted and filthy ejaculations, blaming this girl for all the risks he had to face now — and yet knowing in his heart that an hour ago, from his hallway at 1773, he could have handled the whole thing safely and easily. That misjudgment of his,

179

that open admission, as it were, of his own cowardice and incapacity in all this at the very moment when there had been everything in his favor, became unendurable to him. So he started to curse Eckstrom and McCallister also; and Jane Stewart had to turn the car someway, listening to him, and send it jerking clumsily forward to Parkway Oval.

There was faint light in the sky now, high up, and dark pearly gray; but out on the oval she saw no indication of police activity, just the entry lights gleaming against pale stone, and a mass of shadows tossing in enormous black patches over the park. After they had gone past Eckington Street, but keeping all the way to the far side of the oval, they started back towards it and turned right at the movie theater; and then, two blocks in, the squat modernistic bulk of the Parkway Heights garage could be seen directly in front of them.

Four streets led away from it, under lamp globes crisscrossed one from another at regular intervals; but nowhere in any of these thoroughfares was a police car. Something died in Miss Stewart. She did not know where McCallister and the Lieutenant were, or what kept them elsewhere; but Sheridan did. Two blocks down and one over, he told himself, and still running around in the dark back there on Arlington Drive. Yet he felt no comforting superiority at that idea, but a kind of worried and depressed anxiety, because everything that he saw, or thought of had two faces for him: the thing it seemed to be, now, and thing it might be, actually. He gestured at her with the revolver, the dimples haggard and deeply cut under his prominent cheekbones.

"Up the ramp," he said. "Come on! Don't stop here. Just honk a couple of times, and the guy'll open the door for you. And look." He took his attention long enough from the rear window to whisper these words at her in a grating and deadly undertone. "Did you ever see a man get the brains blown out of his head? Do you want to?"

"Oh, no!" Miss Stewart begged desperately. "No!"

"Then keep your mouth shut," Sheridan directed, settling the Homburg, inching his neck up and around quickly, and putting the gun into his right-hand overcoat pocket. "I'm not getting stopped by him now, or by anyone. I've come too far."

The big overhead door raised up; they drove in, and Sheridan got out of the car and walked around in front of it. She wanted to get out, too, to run from him; but she could not because never once, while talking near the office doorway to the garage attendant, did Sheridan stop watching her. She folded her arms on the steering wheel and put her head into them. Richie, she thought. Richie!

" — sick," she heard Sheridan say. "The wife's old lady. So we're taking her to the hospital, Jack — but in the big car. Back it out for me, will you? And keep this can downstairs for a couple of days. We won't be using it."

Then he took hold of her arm again, guiding her over to a big Buick the garageman was getting into position

181

for them. She was put in behind the wheel, and the door closed after her; and Sheridan walked around the front of it, adding a few words and handing a dollar bill to the garageman, but still watching her. He got in also; the overhead door went up in front of them; and outside it was just as before — no McCallister, no Lieutenant Eckstrom, no anything.

"Back the way we came up," Sheridan said tightly. "Just the way. Go down as far as Eckington Street; but don't turn into it until I tell you." Then he opened the window on his side, pulled the scarf higher around his neck and set the gun in between his knees with the butt low and ready for him.

He had the car now, and the money, the two things which he had wanted and fought for all night; but he understood that the most vital question of all was whether he could still manage to get out of this place before Eckstrom had blocked off every means of escape to him. A few hours ago, when he had been trying to get hold of this girl, Eckington Street had been perfect for him since it was the only one leading east out of the development; but now, and ironically for the same reason, he saw that it might be just as perfect for Frank Eckstrom. He might have covered it first thing, should have; and if he had thought of Eckington Street he would not have forgotten the exit to the West Side Highway that was the only other means of leaving this place by automobile. But had there been time for him to arrange matters? Sheridan did not know, and he could prepare himself only by crouching down and forward against the car door as they approached the Eckington Street corner.

"Pass it slow," he said. "And turn in if I tell you."

A muscle in his throat worked a little, stopped and corded out like thin bone. His heart thumped. And then one block in, placed lengthwise across the first intersection, he saw a police squad car.

He ducked low.

"All right," he said quietly — or perhaps numbly. "Just keep going."

"If he's around here, he's around here," Eckstrom said; "and if he isn't, he isn't." He stood braced solidly on both legs under a corner lamppost on Arlington Drive with McCallister jittering beside him, and with Mahoney and the uniformed cop from 1775 on watch at the other end of the street. "Maybe we'll be able to find him in one of these buildings as soon as we get a little more help from the precinct; but now what we have to do first, McCallister, is to make sure that he doesn't slip out of the development on us. Keep him somewhere in here for the next couple of hours; anywhere. That's our big problem, and that's how I'm handling it."

"If he's around here?" McCallister said, altogether unwilling to admit that it was even a question. "If? He's got to be! He was described, wasn't he?"

"To the life," Eckstrom admitted, as if a little perplexed about that part. "And it's the one thing I can't see, McCallister. What would he be doing in here for hours after the thing happened? Where's the sense to it? What is he after?"

"Yella," McCallister insisted, all nervous energy and impatience now, barely in control of himself. "That's why. He's staked out in some rathole, Lieutenant; and he's afraid to show his nose away from it. Where are those precinct men?"

But it was Gus Bruder who appeared next, shouting breathlessly and waving to them from the cross street that circled down toward Hawthorne Crescent. Then he wobbled up, badly winded after a couple of fast blocks on foot, and blurted in hoarse and effortful gasps at Frank Eckstrom:

"We got it — we got it, Lieutenant! Stein just called the apartment. He located that bartender from Norton's way out in Coney Island someplace, where the guy lives; and the bartender could tell him about the car. It's a dark-green Buick convertible."

Something flashed through McCallister's mind, flickered and then vanished under this new urgency that as yet had no sensible direction; but Eckstrom, after one intent and motionless instant, smashed his hands together and swore passionately.

"So that's it!" he said. "So that's why! Of course! Don't you see it yet, either of you? Didn't you notice the car that was parked all evening on Hawthorne Crescent in front of mine?"

184

McCallister gawked at him. So did Bruder.

"What was I asking?" Eckstrom demanded, that square jaw of his pushing forward quickly and grimly. "Just go back one minute, McCallister. Didn't I want to know why Mr. Sheridan was hanging around here all night? What he was after?"

But of course it was becoming plain then, perfectly plain. McCallister saw it the next moment.

"Trying to get at the car!" he burst out. "And afraid to come near it because he knew that all of us were right upstairs in the house. That's it. That's the only — "

"The only of the only!" Eckstrom said, a ferocious small glitter under his faded and bushy blond eyebrows. "He must have been watching us all the time, and waiting for us to get out of here — and then in the end he had one of Mr. Sheridan's brilliant ideas. He had that garageman move it away for him, out of our sight; don't you remember the fella on the motorcycle that one of you almost knocked over? And a garageman would only take it to a garage for him — so come on now, both of you. That's where we're heading for."

They piled into the coupé, McCallister driving; and on the next corner Jack Mahoney swung on when Eckstrom shouted at him.

"Now," Eckstrom instructed rapidly, "we're going to try to take him from both sides at once, front and back; that's the best way. Slow down at the next corner, McCallister. We'll take the street entrance, but I'll want Bruder and Mahoney to come in at him from the back.

185

Okay. There's a driveway. Use it and keep your eyes open now. And don't let him slip by on you."

They dropped off, running, and McCallister swung left at the next street to the garage ramp.

"Straight up," Eckstrom said, the bass voice deepening noticeably. "In one rush, and before he's able to spot us out here. This time he'll not be able to shoot down better men than himself. But watch it, McCallister. Watch those windows."

It was a wide ramp with a low protecting abutment on each side. McCallister made the turn into it without braking, raced up close against the right-hand wall and slued around just before the entrance in position to block off effectively any desperate plunge from inside by car. He was out then and around the coupé to Frank Eckstrom, who had just kicked the pedestrian door open in the big overhead one.

"Not a sign of him," Eckstrom said hurriedly. "Which means nothing. Come on now. After me, McCallister."

He ducked in, awkward but quick in a half crouch; so did McCallister. They spread out at once, to each side; and the night attendant, who must have heard the coupé screaming up, stopped short just as he reached the office doorway behind them.

"Where is he?" McCallister yelled, watching not the attendant but his side of the garage. "In here? A guy in a Homburg hat and a blue overcoat! Did you see him?"

Mahoney appeared cautiously from the basement

186

level, and McCallister dodged at him past the gas pumps.

"Nothing downstairs," Mahoney explained breathlessly, "but I left Gus there, anyway. In the yard. Do you think we missed him?"

They ran back to the street entrance, where the night man was now beginning a flustered explanation for Frank Eckstrom.

"Well, yeah," he said. "Sure! I picked it up for him like I promised, and then he shows up here and takes it out again. He says his mother-in-law's sick. That he has to — "

"When?" Eckstrom barked. "How long since?"

"Five minutes ago, maybe. Just before you — "

"Closer and closer," Eckstrom declared savagely. "And still missing him. But that's all right. He's in this development now, and we're going to keep him in here if I have to — What's the matter, McCallister? What's wrong with you?"

"That car," McCallister said, in not quite the McCallister voice. He lifted his right arm and pointed it at a brown two-door sedan which he had recognized a moment ago, coldly, as Ed Brady's. "What's it doing in here?"

"They drove up in it," the attendant said. "The guy you're looking for, and this girl he had with him. His wife, I thought."

"With him?" McCallister croaked foolishly. "What girl? Do you mean to say — "

187

"But I didn't know!" the attendant said. "She looked kind of funny to me; but she don't say anything, and I thought that was like he explained, her old lady was sick."

Funny? McCallister thought. His chest had become constricted; he had to gesture twice at Eckstrom before getting some words out.

"But it couldn't be," he said. "I told that cop to put her into the car! To stay with her until — "

It couldn't be; yet it was. He knew that at once by the way Eckstrom took hold of his right arm. "No!" he said. He ran outside, seeing from there only what Miss Stewart had seen earlier, the tall apartment buildings, the empty pavements, the street lamps extending away from him in serene, orderly rows. He ran back. "Lieutenant!" he said. "Lieutenant!"

But there was very little that Eckstrom or anyone else could do for him now.

"Take the coupé," Eckstrom said quietly. "I've got some phoning to do. You can reach me here the minute you get hold of anything; and try that squad car first over on Eckington Street. If he started out that way, McCallister, he'd have seen we were laying for him, and then he'd have kept right on going. So it's possible that they got a glimpse of the Buick. Try them, anyway. And she's all right so far, which means something. There's still a chance."

"But what does he want her for?" McCallister whispered, his flesh ash-colored. "You know, Lieutenant.

Insurance! So that in the end, even if we catch up to him, he'll still be able to — "

"Go on!" Eckstrom said. "Try that squad car. I think there's a good chance they might have spotted him."

McCallister nodded, all hollow-eyed now. He knew Sheridan, and he knew how Sheridan was going to see this — that through the girl, and in the event of his own certain destruction, he could still attain to some kind of triumph over all of them. He careened madly down the ramp, heading straight for Eckington Street but of course precious minutes behind Sheridan and the convertible.

"Who's the girl?" Mahoney said, looking after him. "That nice little nurse, Lieutenant — the one that took care of Paddy?"

Eckstrom nodded. "The same," Eckstrom said. God help her, he thought heavily. He went inside. Jack Mahoney, short and stout as a bull, pursed his lips out, shook his head very slowly from side to side, and then followed him.

Now on Eckington Street that police car still remained in position at the first intersection; and west of this, all the way over on the other side of the development, another car summoned by communicating radio was stationed before the stop sign to the West Side express highway. Three or four men, dispatched hastily from the nearest precinct after Gus Bruder's phone call, had reinforced Eckstrom's first scattered line of defense on the north and east; and one of these, taking his place on top of the railroad embankment, was seen from a big green convertible that turned off immediately, but without obvious or suspicious haste, towards the upper end of Narcissus Road.

Help coming in, Sheridan warned himself; and more on the way — much more. The river behind him; the lots guarded; the roads covered leading out; and on the south, the one direction left him, a massive stone wall that buttressed the development over a college athletic field. A way out there through the cellars, perhaps, or by one of the service entries; but would Eckstrom have overlooked that angle when he had not failed to consider every other?

All his hate and fear of Frank Eckstrom flooded up and blinded him for a moment. That man had not forgotten to start blocking off the development at the very moment when he had learned that Sheridan was inside; and now he would keep it blocked until this was ended one way or the other. He was prepared to let Sheridan move around in it temporarily. Why not? Because minute by minute, section after section, they could drive Sheridan in front of them, constantly narrowing his space for effective maneuver, and all the time throwing in fresh men after him — until at last he was successfully isolated and trapped in some hallway or cellar. Off the streets, he told himself, squeezing his eyes shut for a couple of seconds. But where?

190

"Slow down," he whispered at Jane Stewart. "Stop the car!" She did the only thing she could: what she was told. She bounced one wheel up over the curb on Narcissus Road, banged it down again; and what Sheridan felt for Frank Eckstrom, all the foulness and hate in him, became centered on her.

How did she like it? Sheridan whispered savagely. It wasn't so nice, was it? Running and watching and thinking and trying to — He rubbed his mouth. "But you'll get it before I do," he promised thickly, his lips curling back at her. "That's one thing I'm going to make sure about. So you know the chance you got right now? My chance! Get out of this car!"

She stumbled out somehow, the clumsiness that had made her drive up over the curb spreading itself in a cold, thick wave over what she still hoped for from McCallister and Frank Eckstrom. But how could they find her now? And if they did, how could they get to her before . . . He yanked her on with him into a narrow opening between two buildings; then he stopped there, holding her against him and smoking a cigarette in rapid, agitated inhalations.

"Where were you going?" he demanded of her. "When you got in the car? And don't think it out," he warned, low and dangerous with her at once. "Just tell me. Where were you headed for?"

"To White Plains," she said, her voice muffled. "To my sister's."

So she was out of it, Sheridan realized, so far as they

knew — on her way to White Plains now; there was a chance that McCallister would call her there sometime tomorrow, but certainly no sooner than that. Which meant, from their side, that they had no reason to trouble themselves about her, or about her apartment; and so the apartment had to be it, Sheridan decided hastily. From this point on Narcissus Road, in addition, he could approach 1775 Hawthorne Crescent safely from the rear, and probably get upstairs at this time of night without anybody seeing him. And of course 8E would be empty now; neither Eckstrom nor anyone else would be waiting in there for something to develop when the whole business had apparently popped wide open up on Arlington Drive.

But he went over it once more in order to be quite sure. What was it he needed, all he needed? No more than five or six hours under cover; since at the end of that time, if they had found no sign of him, they would be forced to believe that either the milkman had been mistaken, or that somehow Walter Sheridan had managed to slip out of the development on foot. Tomorrow it should be possible for him to leave entirely unobserved, when people were coming in and out of here by the hundreds; and now, therefore, if he could only scrabble those few tremendously important hours for himself . . .

He made up his mind to it, deciding at once that any risk was worth the acceptance if it gave promise of even a temporary security. Bringing the girl back to the con-

192

vertible with him, he twisted her around against it, whispered orders to remain still at her in a threatening undertone, and unlocked the trunk. Her eyes froze on what she saw in there — a shadowy white face gaping at her, an arm and hand outthrust rigidly. She made a noise in her throat, pulling desperately away from Sheridan; but he got hold of her again and forced her back easily against the fender. She crouched there, unable to move, her eyes darting around helplessly.

There was a suitcase in the trunk also, behind the man. Sheridan pulled that out, and closed and locked everything again. Then he drew her back with him to the alleyway, inspected the street from there, and pushed her up into the shadows ahead of him. A minute went by after they vanished. Another started.

But McCallister, now only a couple of blocks in back of them, because he was rocketing straight ahead on the oval where Sheridan had been forced to take a little time in order to inspect the parkway exit, and to check on a means of escape over the lots, roared up at this moment in front of the squad car on Eckington Street.

"A green Buick convertible!" he shouted. "We found out! Did you see it around anywhere?"

A young cop raced over alertly to him, pointing right down the oval.

"Two minutes ago!" he said. "We were just wondering about it. It slowed up for a second or two, and then — headed that way! You want any help?"

McCallister, however, seemed to release and smash in his gears at the same instant. Everywhere now there was grayness dripping down from the sky, over high roof-tops, and bringing with it an intense early morning hush, remote and brooding. He felt nothing of that. There seemed to be an iron band closing in on the top of his head, tighter and tighter, and from the sick dread that refused now to leave him for even a breath of time he had a taste in his throat that was bone-dry and yet bitter as gall.

All he could think of was Sheridan somewhere with little Miss Stewart. Do what he wants, McCallister tried to tell her, as he had so often, on other nights, counseled her mentally from the living room window in 8E; everything he wants; but don't get him upset, and don't worry him. We'll find him in here; we're right behind him; so if you can only give us the time . . . He felt that he had to get to her now, instantly and somehow; and so he was roaring back towards the oval before the cop had finished speaking to him, under street lights that were turning paler and more colorless with each moment — under a windswept December sky that in the east was now the color of light cocoa.

He saw immediately that there was no convertible on the oval, anywhere on it; and so he raced on into the next cross street. Along that he drove, as far as the lots, stopping and standing erect in the doorway at each intersection to look for the big green Buick; then on again; and at last, the next street down, onto Narcissus Road.

Then back towards the oval, his hands slippery and almost unmanageable on the steering wheel — and then the gleam of a new car ahead of him; a dark-green convertible; a dark-green Buick. He was out and over to it before even thinking of a slow and cautious approach; and the next moment could only stop breathlessly, his heart pounding.

Empty; both doors locked; but the hood still warm! Just missed him, the hood told McCallister; but around here somewhere now — had to be! Where? He sprinted down Narcissus Road to Hawthorne Crescent, abandoning the coupé because Sheridan had abandoned the convertible; he hesitated there; and after a moment's indecision ran into 1775 to see if there was anyone remaining on duty at that point who might have seen or perhaps heard something.

The vestibule was deserted. But Sheridan had reached this building only by a longer and safer route than the direct frontal approach, through the yards; and now the self-service elevator dropped softly into place just in back of McCallister. The door opened, but no one came out. The door slid shut again. The elevator stayed where it was.

McCallister darted over there, his mind reaching for something of the utmost importance, but not quite fitting around it. A small window set at eye level in the door permitted him to see that no one had emerged just now for the simple reason that there was no one inside. He hesitated again. Then why — A row of floor buttons on one wall of the elevator furnished him with the one possible explanation. He backed off. He looked up dumbly. Then from one of the rear apartments on this street level a man wearing trousers and a woolen undershirt reached out for two bottles of milk and his morning newspaper.

"Where's your phone?" McCallister demanded urgently, flashing his badge, pushing the man aside with the same hand, at almost the same instant, and catching sight then of a telephone near the foyer closet.

"Leave your door open!" he blurted out. "Wide open! I have to watch that elevator." Then he had Information on the line, and in half a minute the Parkway Heights garage and Frank Eckstrom.

"I found the car!" he said, sweat beading his eyelashes, and his small head twisting out and around to watch the elevator. "And I think you'd better get over here right away, Lieutenant. He's in this building, I tell you — at 1775. I know! Look. Come in through the yards, so he won't spot you. Yeah, I'll wait. Right in the vestibule."

The male tenant followed him out, scared and yet pleasantly excited by all this. "Who are you looking for?" he asked. "What's going on?" McCallister paid no attention to him. He began to walk up and down, pounding the service revolver into his thigh, and whispering to himself. Upstairs! he thought. Why? What for?

A fury of impatience and helplessness came over him. What had he promised the girl half an hour ago? That Sheridan was nowhere around — that Sheridan was

running, and would keep running. And yet, all the time
. . . Icy coldness gathered inside him. Now he knew
where she was, where Sheridan had her; but would that
help him at all, or help her? Because how, if they trapped
Sheridan upstairs, and if they let him know he was
trapped, could anyone get her away from him before
. . . He put his head into the elevator door, and held it
there. Presently sounds came to him from the basement
laundry room, and Eckstrom's big hat and square
shoulders pushed themselves up out of the stairwell,
Mahoney and Bruder in back of him.

"All right," Eckstrom said stolidly. "What is it? Did
you see him in here?"

"Saw the elevator," McCallister croaked, gesturing
towards it. "His car's up the street; so I run in here to
check on the place; and the elevator comes down empty.
I couldn't have been a minute in back of him! Because
these things stop at the floor where you leave them; if
you get off at eight, they stay at eight until somebody
else rings for them. But this one comes all the way down
here when nobody's ringing for it. Why? Another guy
wouldn't have bothered reaching back and sending it
down again. He'd have left it upstairs. But Sheridan had
another idea. Don't you see? He'd be afraid — "

"Mr. Foxy Sheridan!" Eckstrom said grimly. "That's
our boy, and make no mistake about it. Who saw him
first? The squad car?"

"Of course! That's how I — "

"Then he knew he wasn't getting out of here," Eckstrom said. "Not tonight. Not if we had the roads blocked. They saw him — but he must have seen them, too. Now he must have figured that we don't know anything about that automobile, or we'd have stopped the garageman outside; and that means we shouldn't know anything about the girl, either, because the garage is the one place we could have got some information about her. So I'll tell you what he thought up, McCallister— and I'd put money on it! He's got her up in her own apartment right now, because he thinks he can wait us out from in there till we get tired looking around for him. Do you appreciate the cuteness of it? We think she's left here, and is up at her sister's; so why should we search her apartment? Why should we even think twice about it?"

"Then what are we waiting for?" Mahoney growled, his black eyes small and ugly-looking. "Let's bust in at him! Let's end this thing! That no good, dirty son-of-a — "

"Are you crazy?" McCallister shouted passionately, whirling around. "Bust in at him! And then what'll he do to that girl? He's got her up there, and he'll use her to make some kind of a bargain with us. That's what he'll try! And if we don't listen to him, if we don't let him walk out of here — "

"If?" Eckstrom said. "Use your head, McCallister. We can't listen to him; and you know we can't. Shut up, all of you. I want to think for a minute."

He walked over from them to the street door, and

198

stood there with his hands clasped behind him and his yellow eyes peering out vacantly at Hawthorne Crescent. The citizen watched all this from his apartment doorway, fascinated — Bruder shaking his head, Mahoney angry and baffled, McCallister prowling around, lean, catlike, distracted.

"And I could have stayed with her!" McCallister burst out thickly. "I guess she expected that. But I had to run off and let her — I did it, Gus! Not him. Because I'm the one should have — "

Bruder murmured to him; then no one else said anything until Eckstrom turned back from the street entrance. Even then, however, he had only a question for them, and not a solution.

"Do you think one of us could slip in somehow to that apartment?" he said, addressing McCallister. "He'll be watching and listening at the door, so that's no good; and I guess he'd have the chain on, anyway, so that even the superintendent's key wouldn't help us too much. But the windows up there — How are they placed, McCallister?"

"Just like on our side," McCallister told him, hurriedly visualizing the courtyard wall that he had studied now night after night for three weeks. "First the big picture window in the living room, deepest in; then one in the kitchen; then a small one in the bathroom; then two in the bedroom."

"One on the street," Eckstrom said, blinking thoughtfully ahead of him, "and one on the courtyard. That

199

right? Well, suppose we keep him watching us in our apartment, while someone tried to get in at him through that front bedroom window. That might — "

"Someone?" McCallister said. "Me. Me, Lieutenant!"

"All right," Eckstrom said, nodding at him. "You — if you want it that way. But it's risky, McCallister — because if her rooms are like ours, as you tell me, they run straight out along the courtyard. That means he might see you from the living room, through the bedroom passage — or hear you at the window, unless we can cover you someway. That's the bad part. If he gets any warning, you won't have much of a chance against him. So I'd like you to — "

"What do we do?" McCallister asked quietly. "How do we handle it? That's all, Lieutenant. Just tell me."

There was a white ironwork fernery at the picture window in the 8A living room, a table against the right-hand wall as you looked at this, a couch at the left; and at the two inner corners, one with its back to the Wheeler living room, and the other just in from the foyer, and from the bedroom passage, a couple of easy chairs.

Now, at twenty minutes of six in the morning, Sheridan sat in the one nearest the hall door, with Jane Stewart opposite him in the other. He had the suitcase across his lap, his hands resting loose and relaxed on it, his body slouched back; but whenever she moved at all, or made any sound, the gray eyes were at once open and watching her. The apartment lay hushed around them, with a kind of underwater dimness and strangeness; and out in the courtyard it was still perfectly dark, the windows all black and shiny across from them and not even a kitchen light turned on as yet for an early breakfast.

Sheridan was now completely quiet, and attempting to keep himself completely relaxed. He sprawled low in the chair with his lips pushing in and out, in and out, and with muscles visible in the loose backward arch of his throat when he swallowed every minute or two, in what seemed to be another automatic reaction. At intervals he would observe Miss Stewart silently, and without moving the head, just his eyes; and at these times, with the eyes sunken a bit, but shining at her like steel discs, he had the gauntness and intensity of a physically ill man. His face looked tighter and sharper than ever, even with that sullen outward bulge under his lips; and those long vertical dimples of his, as seen against the shadowy background in here, had taken on the healed bloodless appearance of two surgical scars.

At a quarter of six something happened on the other side of the courtyard. Light sprang up in the living room at apartment 8E, and in slits through the Venetian blind Gus Bruder could be seen screwing an electric bulb into one of the wall sockets. Eckstrom, appearing behind him, took off hat and overcoat, sat down on the cot and with a tired and discouraged gesture rubbed a palm up over each temple. A cop in uniform came in. He said something to Eckstrom. Eckstrom snarled at him. Then the

201

cop appeared to defend himself, and this time Eckstrom got up and bellowed at him. Behind Eckstrom, but still very careful about his actions, Gus Bruder put a finger to his lips and shook his head at the cop in a warning gesture.

None of it seemed quite real to Jane Stewart. There they were, in full sight no more than fifty or sixty feet away from her; and yet for all they could do, or for all they knew about Sheridan, at the antipodes. She bit hard into her lip; and Sheridan, with most of his attention fixed on the picture window in apartment 8E, caught even that almost imperceptible reaction.

"Why don't you yell out?" he suggested softly. "Or get hold of something and throw it into the courtyard. Go ahead. Go on. They'll hear you. And they'll be around to you like a shot."

The flesh under her eyes began to feel hot and swollen. She would not answer him. He backed over to the hall door, listened with his head against it and came back noiselessly.

"Then maybe you're getting some sense," he said. "Keep it up. Sit quiet for a couple of hours in here, watch yourself, and you don't have a thing to worry about. I promise you that — and I ain't a bad kind of guy." He saw the tremor that went over her body. His lips contracted. "Or maybe you think I'm going to bother you," he said. "You!" He studied her with a haggard shadow of his old insolent and contemptuous superiority. "I'll tell you something about my girls, if you want to know.

202

Not your type. Big and fighting, and tough as hell because they don't want to give it to you. That's the way Walter Sheridan gets himself fixed up whenever he needs it. And that's the only way. Big and fighting."

If he doesn't touch me, she thought numbly. If he just doesn't touch me!

"Or maybe you're feeling sorry for yourself." He looked down at her stonily. "Too scared to talk, even. That it?"

"Not any more," she whispered at him, but without looking up. "I think I'm sorry for you."

"Thanks," Sheridan said, softer than ever. "Thanks a lot."

He sat down on the arm of his chair, watching the picture show in 8E — everyone tiptoeing around the great Frank Eckstrom, jumping to attention the minute he snarled at them, just waiting over there to be landed on with both feet. Maybe it all wasn't going too well, eh? A tight, nervous grin crossed his lips, and he inched forward a little, beginning to enjoy this. Then he sprang up suddenly, because out in the kitchen, with a subdued whirr, the electric refrigerator had come on again. Still jumpy, he thought, sweat drenching him. But what for? What did he have to worry about now?

He could not help himself for some reason. He listened again at the hall door, and then looked uneasily down the bedroom passage. Beyond it, a dim gray upright against shadowy walls, he saw the window that looked out over Hawthorne Crescent.

"Come over here," he said. He took her into that room, and examined the street under him, seeing Eckstrom's coupé at the curb, and a couple of uniformed men chatting together near it. Not an idea, he assured himself; not any kind of idea. Still the uneasiness nagged at him. He listened. He heard nothing. He moved back with her, closed the bedroom door after them and locked it. He felt safer that way, as if he had attained to a smaller place, and one even more secret. Across the yard, in 8E, Eckstrom was pounding on in the old Eckstrom routine; he had the milkman from Arlington Drive in there now, and he was berating him, walking up and down in front of him, whirling on him. Go ahead, Sheridan thought tightly; keep it up; and see what it gets you. Just see. . . .

Around the eighth floor at 1775 Hawthorne Crescent there extended an ornamental lip or scallop of gray stone. It was about a foot wide, sloping out and down from the top, and it ran from a small terrace outside the hall window toward the bedroom of apartment 8A, and then past this into the courtyard. It permitted, being situated four feet below the sill, a risky but feasible approach to little Miss Stewart's bedroom; and at this moment McCallister, straddling the terrace rail with his gun stuck in the top of his vest, under his chin, and his hat, shoes and overcoat off, was testing it with one leg while Jack Mahoney held onto him under the armpits.

204

"I don't know," Mahoney whispered anxiously. "It's no kind of a thing to try, Richie; but maybe a couple of us could swing you down from upstairs someway. What do you think?"

Sure, McCallister thought. Ring bells; knock on doors; start the tenants running around; and so let Sheridan know or guess what was happening before there was even a chance at success. He had no desire to argue the matter, or to reason it out; he just wanted to do it. He put both stockinged feet on the ledge, and set his side, one cheek and his two hands flat into the building. "Richie!" Mahoney whispered. "For God's sake!"

He was ignored. Squeezing out onto the ledge, McCallister got his balance there, extended one arm to the window ahead of him, and drew himself over to it quickly but carefully. He felt just one instant of appalling emptiness beneath him; then he was safe at the window, clutching it at each side and facing a bedroom door that was directly ahead of him. The door was closed.

That had been the first big gamble. He let out his breath carefully, balancing himself inward from the toes, and pushed up at the bottom half of the window. It began to give. He nodded over at Mahoney; and Mahoney, twisting back to the hall, made a rapid downward sweep of one hand at a patrolman who was watching him from the elevator turn in the corridor. The patrolman vanished silently. "Okay," Mahoney breathed at him. "Now wait a minute, Richie. Wait till you hear it."

Twenty or thirty seconds passed. In 8E Eckstrom ranted and raged at the milkman; in a back apartment on the eighth floor at 1775, one whose windows could not be seen from any point in the courtyard, the patrolman who had been in the hall just now dialed a number while an excited husband and wife in night clothes fluttered around him; and in the living room at 8A Sheridan nervously put an unlit cigarette into his mouth for some comfort. Wait them out, he kept telling himself. That was all he had to do for a couple of hours. And then tomorrow, when they had been forced to give up on the thing —

The loudest sound he had ever heard in his life came from behind him, from right behind him. It was the 8A telephone. It rang on shrilly, pealing out time after time with Sheridan trying to brace himself against it, but at each repeat feeling another turn of the screw on nerves that already were coiled tight as a hairspring. He saw immediately that Frank Eckstrom was still over there with the milkman, hammering the table at him, roaring; and so it was not Eckstrom. Who then, at this hour of the morning? And why?

"Who is it?" he whispered tensely. "Tell me! Who'd be calling you now?"

"I don't know," Miss Stewart whispered back. She tried desperately to think, that noise jangling in her also with incomprehensible but malicious persistence. Sheridan gripped her by the two shoulders.

"Who is it?"

206

"Maybe the hospital," she told him unsteadily. "I go on duty at seven. You know that. So they'd call if they didn't want me today. That's all I can — "

Sheridan stared down at her. The hospital? he thought, rubbing one side of his face to get some kind of normal feeling into it. No! Never! A trick, rather; a way to . . . He backed off from her to the hall door. But what trick? What were they trying? Groping hurriedly for a logical answer, he looked over again at Frank Eckstrom; then the telephone stopped short, and left aching silence after it. Sheridan tensed uncertainly where he was, the bedroom passage behind him, the bedroom itself no more than eight feet away; and in that bedroom McCallister had just finished slipping himself safe and unheard through the front window.

He rested a moment, shaking helplessly throughout his string-bean body — for the girl, however, not for himself; then he got the gun out of his vest, left the window exactly as it was, and edged forward. There was the possibility that Sheridan might feel a sudden draft of cold air from under the bedroom door; but against this danger was the certainty that, with the telephone silent now, Sheridan would be bound to hear the window being lowered again. So McCallister began to shuffle his way forward on stockinged feet, testing each step carefully before committing his weight to it. The last step or two he was not quite able to breathe. Then the knob took shape under his fingers, and he turned it with steady and exact pressure. Nothing happened, however, when he drew back on it seconds later with his lungs ballooning up painfully in his chest, and with his service revolver laid close into the door before him, and at shoulder height. The door would not open. It was the one Sheridan had closed and locked barely five minutes ago.

"Now," Eckstrom said, speaking to Gus Bruder and the milkman over in the 8E living room, "if one of you looks at that apartment, or blinks his eyes at it, I'll crack his skull open. Where in the hell is McCallister by this time? What is he doing?"

A voice came to him from the corridor door.

"Inside, Lieutenant. Somebody just made the phone call. I think it covered him okay; and I think we're all set."

All set! Eckstrom thought. He began feeling quietly sick. He sat down again at the table, barked something at the milkman, and apparently wrote the answer on a bit of paper. His face was all right, perfectly normal from the other side of the courtyard. His handwriting wasn't.

Across from him in 8A Miss Stewart had closed her eyes for a moment. "You," Sheridan said quietly. "Over here." He had made up his mind to something now; so he moved the gun at her, and she got up without feeling anything much and backed from him into one corner of the foyer. "So you think it was the hospital," he said. She nodded silently. "Okay," he said. "But I think it was them. Let's find out. Get the hospital for me now. Go ahead."

It was a number which she had dialed hundreds of times; but just now she could remember nothing of it, not the exchange, even. "I can't think," she whispered painfully. "You'll have to let me — "

"Then give it here," Sheridan ordered, snatching the phone from her. The garage, he had decided. Where else could they have found out about her, and about him — if they had? He put his gun down and dialed jerkily after Information had got him his number, holding the phone with his other hand and watching her with an icy and hating intentness over the instrument. "I'll get out," he said. "I promised you that, didn't I? But if I don't — " He moistened his lips. "Hello?" he said. "This the garage? Look. I want you to pick up that Buick convertible again. You remember me, don't you? The guy at 1775 Hawthorne Crescent?"

There followed, on the other end of the line, an instant of dead silence.

"What?" the attendant stuttered then. "Sure! But — Wait a minute, mister. Wait just a — "

Sheridan hung up softly. He had caught the change in that voice as soon as he identified himself — the sudden, breathless excitement rising in it. It told him what Eckstrom knew, and how Eckstrom had learned it — through the garage. He rested both hands on the phone and stood that way for a moment with the muscles around his tight straight mouth jumping and quivering.

209

So they had stumbled onto the garage, somehow; they had found out about the convertible; they had located it downstairs, probably; and they had just called him here on the phone to see if he'd be stupid enough to answer them. And where were they now? All through the building, of course; all scattered around through it; all waiting for him.

No way out, Sheridan understood then; not from this. He looked up at the girl, the one who had started everything, who had trapped him now, in the end, as she had involved him first in the beginning. This was the thing he must do now, Sheridan remembered. Hadn't he promised her? Hadn't he, in his heart, promised all of them? He moved silently around the foyer table, and Miss Stewart, seeing what was in his face, backed from him just as silently into the corner. No! she thought. Oh, no! Richie!

But McCallister was still on the other side of that bedroom door. He was, in fact, leaning out the front window overlooking the crescent, and Mahoney was leaning over towards him from the hall terrace. They could have touched hands; but there was as yet no reason to do that. "It's on the way!" Mahoney whispered at him. "Easy, Richie. Take it easy! I'll see if — "

He vanished. And then there was nothing for McCallister to do, nothing at all, but to crouch there second after second after second, watching the terrace. He felt empty. Then he felt physically nauseated. He put his head on the window sill, rolled it there, prayed dumbly

— and saw Mahoney, pale and excited, again reaching out to him, but this time with the superintendent's passkey.

He was at the bedroom door with it when he heard the first sound of any description from the living room — the girl's voice muffled, panicky, then the lurch and shuffle of quick bodily movement. Careful, McCallister warned himself frantically; because now, in these next few moments — The lock clicked sharply, despite his efforts. He sobbed a little. Then he yanked the door open and squeezed through, and straight ahead of him, in the one spot where McCallister had prayed he would be, saw Sheridan's white face spinning blindly to him.

Halfway between them, and visible in this watery dimness as the faintest glimmer of shaped metal, lay the big service revolver where Sheridan had set it down just before making his call to the Parkway Heights garage. Each of them became aware of it at the same moment — McCallister with an inward explosion of savage and exultant triumph, Sheridan with the sickness and shock of naked physical panic.

There was of course nothing said, nothing asked or given between them. Sheridan, paper-white in that shadowy foyer, lunged down and back for the gun, his one chance; while McCallister, already in blurring motion from the bedroom doorway, came all the way at him in one headlong and driving plunge. He hit Sheridan at chest height, smashing him back over the foyer table; but even then, while sliding away from it, and going

211

down with McCallister on top of him, Sheridan clutched somehow, in a groping and sidewise motion, onto the service revolver.

There was no opportunity to bring it around, however. The table splintered and cracked under them; they rolled over it; then they landed side-to-side on the floor behind it, the gun up against the wall with Sheridan holding the barrel end, the wrong end, and with McCallister's two hands pinning the gun in that position.

They appeared to churn slowly and clumsily for a moment, Sheridan's right arm, under McCallister's shoulder, helpless also, and his left twisting away from him, as if of itself, as McCallister braced and extended both of his hands against it. Sheridan groaned painfully. "No!" he breathed. "McCallister! McCallister!" Then his fingers were spread apart, and the revolver dropped away from them, and he became quite still with both his eyes squeezed shut and the muscles on the visible side of his throat corded out under the flesh like chunks of wire.

"Open the door," McCallister panted up at Jane Stewart, who had been all this time standing frozen over them. "It's okay — I got him now. And I think the Lieutenant's out there waiting."

"End it," Sheridan whispered at him. His head, the only part of him he could move, rolled into the wall and back toward McCallister with an impression of anguished and enormous physical effort. "For Christ's sake, McCallister! I worked with you. End it now!"

212

But then Eckstrom was in from the outside corridor, and Jack Mahoney, and a couple of uniformed men.

"You bastards!" Sheridan sobbed at them. "You lousy bastards!" He opened the gray eyes, screaming this up at the faces over him, and that was the way McCallister remembered him later, the whole face glistening, the eyes shrinking away from them after that first look — sick, lost — the voice wailing desolately in their ears. "Can't you end it for me? Lieutenant!"

But Eckstrom was regarding him silently, and without expression.

"Not so easy," Eckstrom said then, in that raspy and tough-sounding voice of his, "and not so quick. All right, McCallister. Get him up."

The last police car pulled away from Hawthorne Crescent at a few minutes before seven. McCallister watched it go from the picture window in the empty and deserted living room of apartment 8E, Ahern's pipe tobacco still lying on the sill beside him, and December sunlight out in the courtyard sparkling and shining, with the roof shadow of 1775 outlined cleanly across floor after floor in one bold downward stroke. He looked tired now. He felt tired. It seemed oddly quiet in the apartment with nobody else there, and inside of him he was conscious of nothing but emptiness and exhaustion. He did not know where to go. He could not think of anything he had to do. Then, at five minutes past seven, two of Eckstrom's day shift came in and eyed the back of his head quietly, tentatively, as if aware that they ought to say something to him, but without being in any way sure as to what it should be.

One of them cleared his throat finally.

"About Paddy," he said, looking faintly embarrassed. "I guess you know how we feel about him, Richie. We just heard downstairs. But what's there to say?"

"That's it," McCallister said, not turning immediately. "What?"

He hefted the pipe tobacco, tossed it up a couple of times and caught it.

"His own worst enemy," the second man said, ponderously solemn about that statement. "But one hell of a nice guy, Paddy Ahern. Everyone liked him."

"They had to," the first one said. "That's one thing you got to admit — they had to."

McCallister said nothing. There was a short, awkward silence.

"Well," the first one said, "I guess we're about through here. We were just told to lock up the joint, Richie. Anything around here you want? Anything you're forgetting?"

McCallister put the pipe tobacco back carefully on the window sill. "I guess not," he said. He nodded at them, went out to the hall, closing the door after him, and noticed half a dozen people gathered together near one of the apartment doorways. They stopped their conversation at once, watching him curiously but covertly as he rounded the turn up from them and passed along the other end of the corridor to the last door on his right, to apartment 8A. He rapped there.

This time she wore a neat blue dress with a wide and frothy white collar on it, but even at that she didn't appear to be quite herself to McCallister — a bit too pale, a little too shadowed and fatigued-looking around those brown eyes. He gave her his usual solemn nod.

"I thought I'd drive you up," he said. "To White Plains. Or put you into a taxi, anyway. You're going now, aren't you?"

She flushed, perhaps a little ashamed of herself.

"Yes," she admitted. "I think so. I think I'd better."

"Me, too," McCallister, said, studying her soberly. "And look. You've got to start using your head now. You don't want to go over and over what happened tonight. You want to forget it."

"Yes," she said. Her mouth twisted around the least bit. "Oh, yes, Richie. I know that. And you, too."

"Me?" McCallister said, speaking in a dry, light tone, as if that angle had not struck him before. "I'm okay. Only I can't seem to believe it about Paddy just yet. I keep thinking that he's around somewhere. That tonight when I — "

"Will you wait for me?" Jane Stewart said, at just the right point, just as he set his teeth together. "Or come in. I won't be a second."

He'd wait, McCallister thought, lighting a cigarette he

did not want particularly. But he wouldn't forget Paddy like that, no matter what anybody said; he wouldn't forget him ever.

They walked back to the elevator, McCallister carrying her overnight things, and the citizens all fell silent again near the turn, so that McCallister felt his lips tightening up helplessly on him.

"Well, why don't you ask me?" he demanded, sudden and savage with them, and swinging around immediately after he had jammed his thumb on the elevator signal button. "You want to; so go ahead. I'll tell you about the cop that got killed. I'll tell you about as good and decent a guy — "

"Richie," Jane Stewart said. It all went out of him.

"Okay," he said, very low. "Okay." Then the elevator appeared and they rode down in it without speaking again. But out in the courtyard, where there was sunlight and sharp wind, everything bright, cold, different and magical out there, she took his arm and held it under her own, close to her.

"It won't last," she said. "You'll see, Richie. Not like this, anyway. And come to see me. Come soon."

"Sure," McCallister said, but without really thinking about it. "Thanks. I'll do that."

He found a cab out on the oval, put her into it, nodded again, took off his hat.

"Don't forget," she said, very earnest there. "Please, Richie."

After this she went off in the cab, and McCallister got

that queer feeling again — nowhere to go, nothing to do. He glanced back at 1775; old Paddy, he thought quietly; then he turned, any direction at all, and had a glimpse of her taxi bobbing away from him down Eckington Street.

He walked off after it with long, nervous strides, feeling the other thing in his heart now, the way it had to be for a while between him and Paddy. And with her? Soon, he remembered, raising his small head quickly. Very soon. Of course. But not just yet.